**"Do you** [believe in life]
**after dea**[th, Mr. Graham?"]

"I think it's possible."

"Then isn't it also possible that this man, who has been set up, framed by people he thought were his friends, accused of a terrible crime and then assassinated himself—isn't it just possible his essence, or personality, or *psyche*, as the Greeks called it, might return to a place that he associates with a turning point in his life on Earth?"

"You're saying that there was a conspiracy to kill Kennedy and that Oswald wasn't involved except as a dupe."

Fontenot nodded slowly, his eyes hard on mine.

"Then what does the dam project have to do with it all?"

"The land will be flooded. The cabin will be taken down."

"And?"

"The spirit will have nowhere to go. Don't you see?" He leaned close to me then. "The only one who can bring it all to light is the ghost: Lee Oswald's spirit. They have to destroy that. They have to kill Lee Oswald again!"

Avon Books are available at special quantity discounts for bulk
purchases for sales promotions, premiums, fund raising or educa-
tional use. Special books, or book excerpts, can also be created to
fit specific needs.

For details write or telephone the office of the Director of Special
Markets, Avon Books, Inc., Dept. FP, 1350 Avenue of the
Americas, New York, New York 10019, 1-800-238-0658.

# ASSASSIN'S BLOOD

## AN ALAN GRAHAM MYSTERY

## MALCOLM SHUMAN

AVON

TWILIGHT

This is a work of fiction. Names, characters, places, and incidents either are the product of the author's imagination or are used fictitiously. Any resemblance to actual events, locales, organizations, or persons, living or dead, is entirely coincidental and beyond the intent of either the author or the publisher.

AVON BOOKS, INC.
1350 Avenue of the Americas
New York, New York 10019

Copyright © 1999 by Malcolm K. Shuman
Inside cover author photo by Thomas A. Wintz, Jr.
Published by arrangement with the author
Library of Congress Catalog Card Number: 99-94803
ISBN: 0-380-80485-9
**www.avonbooks.com/twilight**

First Avon Twilight Printing: September 1999

AVON TWILIGHT TRADEMARK REG. U.S. PAT. OFF. AND IN OTHER COUNTRIES, MARCA REGISTRADA, HECHO EN U.S.A.

Printed in the U.S.A.

WCD 10 9 8 7 6 5 4 3 2 1

*This is for Darwin Shrell,*
*scholar and friend*

# Acknowledgments

The author owes a great deal to several people. Chiefly, he is grateful to his editor, Jennifer Sawyer Fisher; to her assistant, Clare Hutton; and to the entire staff at Avon Books. He is also appreciative of the efforts of his agent, Peter Rubie, and of the continuing support of his wife, Margaret.

# ▰PROLOGUE

It was just after noon, and the crowd was already gathering below in Dealey Plaza. The thin, sharp-faced young man, however, was uninterested in the excitement. Instead, he lounged nonchalantly against the wall of the cluttered sixth-floor area, a smirk on his face, his eyes on the corner of the building and its big window.

They'd all gone to lunch, leaving him here alone. Soon he would do what had to be done.

The elevator door opened, and he wheeled around as one of his co-workers got off.

"You seen my cigarettes?" the man asked. "I could swear I left 'em."

The younger man shrugged. Then his visitor saw the pack of smokes on a packing crate, picked them up, and stuck them in his pocket.

"Boy, are you going downstairs?" the visitor asked.

"No, sir," the younger man answered.

"Suit yourself," the other said with a shrug and got back onto the elevator.

Only when the elevator began to move again did the young man spring into action.

He dragged cardboard boxes of books across the plywood floor, making a three-sided enclosure on the southeast corner so that no one leaving the elevator would be able to see him. Then he retrieved the brown paper bag he'd secreted here earlier.

Curtain rods, he'd told his neighbor about the oblong

1

*package. And his neighbor, who had driven him to work, had accepted the explanation.*

*Curtain rods.*

*The young man laughed and ran a sweaty palm through his short, dark hair.*

*It would be over soon. And there wouldn't be another miss, like when he'd shot at the general in April. This time he would use sheer willpower to quiet the butterflies in his belly.*

*He stripped away the newspaper, hands trembling as the outline of the bolt-action rifle revealed itself.*

*He fitted the stock and action together, pulled back the bolt, and screwed the four power scope to the top. Then he loaded the clip with four cartridges, each a man killer.*

*In the distance he heard sirens echoing into the plaza and off the buildings.*

*He opened the window and, twisting the sling around his arm, rested the rifle on the sill and sighted through the scope.*

*A young woman in a red dress was standing on the far curb, and with a quick turn of the adjustment knob he brought her round face into focus.*

*It was a pleasant face, slightly anxious, as if she wasn't sure she had time to spend here and wished the procession would hurry and arrive. How easy it would be to kill her right now. Just a squeeze of the trigger, and her head would explode in a halo of red.*

*But she wasn't his target. His target was someone infinitely more important. Someone stupid women like that one pretended to admire, as if he were God Almighty. It was disgusting, because the man who would be driving by in a moment was no different than anybody else, just born rich, as if wealth conferred some kind of sainthood.*

*The sirens were loud now, blasting into the plaza, and he swung the rifle barrel toward the far edge just in time to see the first motorcycle policeman.*

*The gunman's heart was pounding now so loud he was sure that if anyone else had been up here with him they would have heard it.*

*Thirty seconds, and all the past failures of his life would be erased. Thirty seconds . . .*

*He swung the barrel back to the street below and swore to himself at the tree branches that blocked his view.*

*He'd have to fire quickly, before the limo reached the tree. And his shot would have to count. Because if he missed, he'd have to fire through a break in the foliage, which was trickier.*

*The sirens were right under him now, and he pressed his eye against the scope.*

*Suddenly he saw it, the black open limo, with the governor in the front and his target, wearing a dark suit, in the seat directly behind.*

*His target was waving.*

*He took a deep breath, brought the crosshairs steady on the president's head, and pressed the trigger.*

*That was how I imagined the assassination of John Fitzgerald Kennedy thirty-six years ago. A third of a century before I went to Jackson. A third of a century before the other deaths . . .*

# ONE

Pepper was gone. She had gotten up early one morning in April, and I had driven her to the airport in New Orleans. Two hours later she was on a plane to Mexico.

Working at the Maya site of Lubaanah was too great an opportunity to pass up. Working with Eric Blackburn was just an added plus.

Blackburn was married with children, and despite his calculatedly rakish appearance, it was ridiculous to think of anything developing between them.

She and I had worked together for two years, had almost been killed a few times, and had finally become lovers, despite a ten-year difference in our ages. Nothing would change the way she felt, not even an archaeologist her own age with a half-million dollars from *National Geographic* to study Maya trade relations in the early historic period.

"It's just that we both need some time," she'd explained. "It's only four months, and you can fly down and visit."

I promised I would. And lied.

I'd had a bad experience in Mexico years before, when I'd met a beautiful Mexican archaeologist on a dig in Yucatán. We'd ended up married, but our careers had brought us into conflict. I'd gone round the bend, lost my university position, and come back to Baton Rouge to do contract archaeology. I was just getting my emotions together when I met Pepper. She'd given me something I'd never expected to have again. But I didn't know if I was ready for Mexico and its memories.

And she may have known. There were still things about her I didn't understand, and when she'd announced her intention to go, I sensed that it was our closeness that frightened her as much as her professed desire to jump into a field in which she had no previous experience.

"You don't even read Maya," I said.

She told me she'd learn.

That was a month ago, and I'd gotten one lousy letter before they'd disappeared into the jungle.

Now I felt an emptiness, even a betrayal. I plunged into work. One day our Corps of Engineers contracting officer, Bertha Bomberg, A.K.A. La Bombast, called and told us she was sending us to inventory the archaeological sites along a stretch of Thompson Creek, thirty miles to the north.

The Corps was thinking of building a dam and flooding a few thousand acres of pine forest. The plan was touted as a way to draw tourists for fishing and recreation, but everyone knew it would really benefit the politicians who had bought up most of the land.

I pulled into the tiny community of Jackson at just after nine. It was a warm May morning, with summer hiding in the shadows of the old buildings. In a few weeks the blackberries would be ripe. Idyllic, if you didn't have to beat your way through the berry patches in hundred-degree heat.

The man I'd come to meet was waiting in a pickup next to the bank. He got out as I approached, a round little fellow of fifty in a short-sleeved shirt and cowboy boots, who looked happy with the world.

"Dr. Alan Graham?" He came forward with his hand outthrust. "Gene McNair. I own the eastern half of the tract. I'm also on the board of the Development District."

We shook and he nodded over his shoulder.

"You been to Jackson before, right?"

"Just for pleasure," I said, and he cracked a grin. The state mental hospital is in Jackson.

"Well, it's a nice little town. Been around since the middle of the last century. Used to be a center for cotton shipping. Railroad took the cotton west to the Mississippi for loading onto boats. This was a hopping place back then: Centenary College was the first institution of higher learning in the state. Asphodel Plantation, down the road, was built in the early 1800s. It's on the National Register, you know.''

I nodded.

"We're trying to get things started up again. Get known for something besides a mental hospital and a correctional institution.''

"You have a lot of local backing?'' I asked.

"Everybody except one or two. But that's always the way it is.'' He folded his arms. "Look, if you found an Indian grave, would that hold things up?''

"Probably. The state has a strong burial law. Any human remains have to be reported to the authorities within twenty-four hours, and then if they're Native American, interested tribes have to be given a chance to comment. So I imagine it would slow things down. But most of what we find isn't burials. Mostly it's Indian artifacts—projectile points and pottery—and old house remains from the last century. If we find something that seems important, then we have to recommend what to do with it.''

"Like excavate?'

"That or avoid it completely.''

"Sounds interesting,'' McNair said dubiously.

I nodded. Most people said what I did was interesting, whether they believed it or not.

I left my red Blazer in the lot and climbed into McNair's pickup, and a few seconds later we were heading north on a winding two-lane. To the left was a terrace, with the creek at the bottom. The creek had etched its way into the landscape during the last Ice Age, which ended ten thousand years ago. The hills were made out of loess, a fine clay that the glaciers had ground into a dust a thousand miles to the north and deposited here on the winds. It was a good place to find fossils, with a better than average chance of turning up leavings of the first Americans, who had come here just before the Ice Age ended.

Three miles from town we turned left onto a dirt road,

dipping down toward the valley across a pasture. Five minutes later we came to an iron-bar gate, and McNair hopped out with a key and unlocked it.

"I'll give you a key when we finish today," he said. "From here on down to the creek is my land."

We shot through the gate and started winding downward.

"The other half of the tract you need to look at is on the other side of the creek, in West Feliciana. That belongs to the Devlins. To get to my land, you come up Highway 952 on this side of the creek. To get to the Devlin tract, you go up Highway 421, that runs parallel to it on the other side. The creek's the dividing line between the two tracts, and it's the parish line, as well."

A deer leaped out in front of us and then bounded away, its flag high.

"Damn, I wisht it was hunting season," my guide swore.

"Are the Devlins a problem?" I asked.

"Just the one that lives there. Real pain in the ass."

"He's against the project," I said.

"*She*. Cynthia Jane, but everybody calls her Cyn. She was okay before her husband died. But ever since, well, I think it knocked a screw loose. I don't think she'll shoot at you, though."

"She lives by herself?" I asked.

"Yeah, in a big-ass old house on Highway 421. But her land only goes about halfway back to the north." Gesturing with his head he said, "Across the creek there belongs to her brother-in-law, Buck, but she's against his selling. You'd think it was her own family's land instead of his."

We came to the edge of the terrace. The road ended here, and somebody had thought it was a good vantage point for hunting, because a wooden deer stand had been built onto an oak tree on the right. I looked over the edge of the bluff and down at the creek. It was a shallow, sandy expanse a hundred feet wide, with the water in pools and very little current. A wooden stake with a red ribbon guarded the end of the road, and I pointed.

"Are the perimeters staked?"

"Supposed to be."

"And this Devlin woman let the surveyors onto her land?"

"Raised hell, but what can she do? The state'll expropriate if it has to."

I nodded. I hated these kinds of situations.

"Can we get across here?" I asked.

"If you don't mind getting your feet wet."

I got out of the truck and followed him to the clay bank, then slid down to the sandy beach. We sloshed through the water, came up onto a sandbar, sloshed some more, and emerged on the other side. At least there were no POSTED signs. The pine hills rose up in front of us, but to the left was a narrow jeep track. I made for it, McNair breathing hard behind me.

The aerial photos hadn't shown many clear-cuts, which were hell in the summer because of the thick briars, but I needed to get a feel for the topography and especially the amount of undergrowth so I could put together a cost estimate.

"You're the first archaeologist I heard of who didn't work at a college," McNair said, puffing behind me.

"Actually," I said, reaching the top of the hill, "most archaeologists don't work at universities. Most do just what I do, contract archaeology. It's a new field that developed from the environmental movement of the sixties. When they made laws to protect the wildlife, they decided it would be a good idea to protect historical sites, as well."

The track entered the trees a few yards ahead of me, and I started forward, the pine needles soft under my boots. In the ruts I saw some raccoon prints and then some deer droppings, but there was no sign that humans had been this way in the last few weeks.

"Where does this track go?" I asked.

"To a clearing up ahead with an old camp house. Then it goes south, into the back pasture of the Devlin place."

"Is this camp house very old?" I asked.

McNair gave a little laugh. "Nah. Built in the fifties. But you don't want to go there."

"No?" I was already in the forest, and I saw a patch of sunlight ahead through the trunks. "Why's that?"

"Might stir up the tenant."

"Somebody lives there?" I could see the building now, a wood-frame structure with a tin roof. The windows were broken and the front porch sagged. "They don't keep it up very well, if they do."

"Well, they don't really live there—they just haunt it."

"What?"

He gave a high-pitched laugh. "That's just the teenagers around here. They call it Lee's Place."

"Lee?"

"Lee Harvey Oswald. They say he stayed here just before he killed Kennedy. Some say his ghost is still here and that's why bad things happen to people who come on this land."

# ≡Two

"Oswald?" I asked.

"It's just the kids making things up. But it's a fact he came here just about three months before JFK got killed. Said he was looking for work at the hospital. Came to Jackson and then went over to Clinton, the parish seat, to talk to a state senator. Must not've found anything, because he left and went back to New Orleans. But lots of people saw him, and he gave his name, because he was trying to register to vote so he could get a job in the parish."

"How's he connected to this cabin?"

McNair shrugged. "Damned if I know. Maybe 'cause the cabin's lonesome and kinda spooky. The kids come across the creek the way we did—they wouldn't dare come through Cyn's property."

I walked up to the cabin and gingerly tried the porch. There was a wasp nest over the door, but it was old and dried up. I pushed the door open slowly and looked inside.

The interior was dim and smelled of dust. I remembered when I was a kid in Baton Rouge and how other kids told stories about a mysterious ball of fire that seemed to appear in the swamps near the town of Gonzales, twenty miles down the road. Nobody had ever seen it, but everybody knew somebody else who had.

I turned around and stepped back onto the ground.

"Okay, Mr. McNair. I guess we can go back."

\* \* \*

I returned to Baton Rouge and the big wooden frame house across from the campus in Tigertown, where we had our offices and lab. We called ourselves Moundmasters, because we'd dug into so many of the damned things, and it had more character than the names some of our competitors chose, like Pyramid Research. There were just myself; an ex-rabbinical student named David Goldman, who had dropped Talmudic studies for playing in the dirt; Marilyn Fisk, our tiny bookkeeper and factotum; Frank Hill, who was working on his master's; and some temporaries, who ground out reports on a couple of PCs and sorted artifacts in the big living room we called the lab. My office was a room at the back, with a plywood partition, notices and deadlines dangling from all the walls, and a bookcase at one side. The desk, which I'd picked up at a yard sale, was piled with reports to review and bits and pieces of proposals in progress.

The next couple of weeks I spent on other projects and in writing the cost proposal for the Jackson work. I also had to recruit a crew, which was easy since it was summer and there were university students eager for work. Then I faxed Bombast the cost estimate and waited.

When she called to negotiate the cost, I knew it was going to be one of those days. It took two hours, but finally we agreed on all items.

When he heard me hang up and sigh, David crept into my office.

"We okay?"

I nodded. "But she cut us back on time in the field and report prep."

"At least we have the job."

I sighed. "Yeah, but I hate it when the argument ends with her saying, 'I'm the government.' "

"Maybe she was talking about size. When do we hit the field?"

"She said a week. So make it two."

"Good. I could stand getting out from under these reports. And you"—he folded his arms—"could stand to get your mind off Pepper Courtney."

"I know." I got up and turned around to face him. "David, what do you know about Lee Harvey Oswald?''

"Oswald? Forget it, man. He's dead. You'll have to hire somebody else to take care of Bombast.''

"Seriously. Ever read anything about the Kennedy assassination?''

He leaned against the wall.

"I saw the movie. I thought it was a lot of bullshit, though. Why?''

I told him about the local lore I'd picked up in Jackson.

"It's funny the way stories get started. But he apparently did go to Jackson once, not long before he left New Orleans for Dallas, and people remembered.''

"Yeah, I think I read something about that in the paper once. I bet everybody's got a story about the day he came to town, like Jesse James robbing the bank.''

I sat on the edge of my desk, crushing a stack of papers.

"They say everybody in the country who was old enough to think can remember where they were when Kennedy was shot. I know I do. I was ten, in the fourth grade. We were at phys ed, playing flag football, and I saw one of the teachers, Miss Daigle, talking to Coach Mapes. I'd been in a scrape in her class that morning, and I knew she was telling him to call me over. The whistle blew, and I started over to the sidelines. I was already getting my story ready. I walked right up to them and then I saw she was crying and I wondered how I could have made her do that. Then she turned and walked away, and I asked Coach what was the matter. He just looked at me like I wasn't there and said, 'The president's been shot.' ''

I got up from the desk. "When I was growing up, I just naturally thought there had to have been other gunmen. But then, while I was in graduate school, there was an archaeology convention in Dallas, and I walked down to Dealey Plaza. I remember looking up at the Book Depository and then at the road and the buildings on the other side, and thinking, 'Everything is so much smaller than it looks in the pictures. One man really *could* have made that shot.' And that's what I still think. But I've never quite understood why he did it.''

"He was screwed up.''

"Yeah."

I walked out into the lab, where one of our student workers was trying to fit together the fragments of an ancient Indian bowl. She had already glued six or seven big pieces in place, so that the delicate curve of the neck was plain, but most of the rest of the vessel lay in bits on the table. Sometimes you managed to get the whole thing together, but more often you were left with blank spots.

The next morning I drove back to Jackson. I wanted to talk to a man named Clyde Fontenot, whose name had been given me by McNair as the closest thing to a town historian. When the project got under way, our own historian, Esmerelda LaFleur, would have to write a historical background of the area and check land titles, and I wanted to find out whether Fontenot would be a good source for her to interview for the local history.

Clyde Fontenot's house was a bungalow on the outskirts of town, but his wife, a gray-haired woman of fifty, said he was downtown at the barber shop. She said it like everyone in town knew to look for him there. When I found the barber shop, I saw why.

Sandwiched between two wooden buildings with historical markers, the tiny brick structure looked out on Highway 10 through a dusty window with a diagonal crack. A couple of men lounged in chairs along the wall, while the barber sat in his own chair, a cigarette in his hand. When I came in, he got up.

" 'Morning," he said, reaching for the sheet.

I said I was looking for Mr. Fontenot, and one of the men along the wall stood.

"That's me." He was skinny and not much over five feet, with thick glasses that made him look like a frog and eyes that projected like flags. He stuck out a hand and we shook.

I told him why I'd come. "And I hear you know a lot about the history of this area," I finished.

He chuckled and scratched his head. "Well, I write columns for the *News-Leader*. I used to be a teacher at the high school here. Anything special you wanted to know?"

"Well, if there are any Indian sites or historical sites of

any kind on the tract they're going to use for the dam . . .'' I began.

"There's a big Indian site over on Fee Hudson's farm," the barber said. "Busted rocks all over the place."

"That isn't what the man asked," Fontenot said, turning to me. "You know about that site already, don't you?"

"There's a mound on Ethyl Road," the other kibitzer said. "A hundred feet high at least. Biggest thing I ever saw."

"Dewey, that's a damned hill," Fontenot said. "Indians never made that thing." He turned to me. "Did they?"

"A hundred feet's pretty big for it to be man-made," I said.

"*We* always called it an Indian mound," Dewey said, chagrined.

"Well, I don't cut hair and Gus doesn't sell postage stamps," Fontenot chuckled.

"Hell with you," Dewey said and folded his arms.

Gus said, "Adolph here's the assistant postmaster. Spends most of his time opening other folks' mail. I don't know what Clyde is. Mainly he just sits around here and bothers folks."

Adolph Dewey said, "Mister, do me a favor and take both of 'em."

Clyde gave a guffaw. "I think you got mail to sort. But I'll be happy to go with this gentleman."

He proved to be an excellent guide with a deep knowledge of both the parish and the town itself. First we drove out to the Indian site, which, while not on the tract to be surveyed, deserved to be reported. We collected stone artifacts from the top of a ridge. I took pictures while Fontenot watched approvingly and discussed the history of French-Natchez relations and the Fort Rosalie massacre. I'd run into many like him in small towns: knowledgeable and intelligent, but without equals to talk to. It could be a lonely existence, but Clyde seemed contented enough, rattling on about the Houmas and their move south along the river, as the result of European pressure, to their present place in Terrebonne Parish near the Gulf.

When we finished, we had a nice collection of points and scrapers and a couple of flint knives.

Afterward he showed me where Cyn Devlin lived. It was a mile and a half north of town, but on the west side of the creek that was the parish boundary. The house itself was an 1890s-vintage mansion that sat a hundred yards back from the road in a grove of hickories with a gazebo to one side.

Even from the highway I could see that the paint needed touching up in places and the gazebo could stand to have its latticework repaired.

There was a station wagon in the drive, and I wondered if the lady herself was at home.

"What does Miss Devlin do?" I asked.

My guide laughed. "Not much, far as I can tell. But I've always gotten along with her. I taught her son, Mark, before I retired. Sad business."

"What's that?"

"Bright kid. But he got killed in a traffic accident on US 61 a couple of years ago. He was just sixteen years old. Then, just last year, her husband, Doug, died right across the creek from the Devlin place. Shot by some poacher. Nobody ever got caught. Cyn's had her share of trouble, and she isn't even forty."

"I hear she's against the dam. Think it has anything to do with her husband's death?"

"Don't see how. She's against it because it won't do anything but ruin the land and make some crooks rich. Some are saying she's crazy. Well, we need more crazy people like her."

"Can't she just tie it all up in court?"

"Not that simple. The land belonged to her husband's family. Cyn isn't from around here. When old Timothy Devlin died in 1980, the land got split between his two sons, Buck and Doug. Now Buck was off in the Army and gave a power of attorney to his younger brother, Doug. Doug had the house and the back pasture, and Buck took the woods to the north—told folks he didn't figure to live here anyway. Then Doug got killed, and a few months later Buck came back. Of course, the power of attorney ended when Doug died. Buck lives in Baton Rouge now, but I hear he's willing to sell. Cyn's mad as a wet hen, but there isn't much she can do.''

I turned around and headed back toward Jackson.

"Tell me about some of the other people involved," I said. "Gene McNair owns the land on the east side of the creek, in this parish."

"Right. The land where Doug got killed. Bought it two years ago right after the election, as quiet as a mouse. Got it from Sam Pardue for a song, before anybody'd whispered a word about this dam.''

"How does Pardue feel?"

"Like killing all the McNairs. But what can he do? His daddy got it at a sheriff's sale during the Depression. All he was using it for was as a lease to a hunting club.''

"What's Gene McNair got to do with all this?" I asked.

Clyde waved a hand disparagingly. "Gene isn't anything but a flunky for his brother, Buell. Buell's a state senator, in tight with the crooks that stand to make a fortune on this thing.''

I started to ask him about the Oswald story but changed my mind. It was only the folklore of high school kids, so why bother?

I dropped him at his house, where his wife came out to stand on the porch and watch to see that he came in, as if he might get away, and I drove back out to the old Pardue tract.

McNair had given me a key, and I opened the iron gate and drove through.

I wasn't sure what I was looking for. I'd seen the tract already, and there were things I had to do in Baton Rouge.

Maybe it had something to do with the idea of a man lying dead on the same ground I had walked over. Or maybe it had to do with the dilapidated little cabin that now belonged to the dead man's brother but was linked in the folklore to another dead man, who formed a dark vortex in our national history.

I came to the tree with its deer stand and gazed out over the valley, trying to envision how the area would look with the water lapping at my feet.

Clyde Fontenot was right. The dam was a cockamamie idea in a state noted for such notions.

I reached into a patch of briars and plucked a couple of blackberries. They were thick and sweet now, ready for the picking. In another two weeks they would start to dry from the sun. I thought about the blackberry cobblers my mother made when I was little. In those days you could drive five miles from town and find the berries alongside the roads. That had long since changed, with the blooming of the chemical industry and the fencing of lands.

I turned to go and heard a splashing below me. I wheeled, expecting to see a deer, but instead it was a man. It was too far for me to get a good look at him, but he was white, wearing a checked shirt and jeans, and I couldn't help suspecting that he'd chosen the second my back was turned to make for the other side of the stream.

He reached the other side and started up the trail at a fast walk toward the cabin. I thought of calling out, but there was something furtive about him that made me hesitate. Instead, without weighing the decision, I followed.

By the time I was at the stream's edge, he had vanished into the forest above, and as I slopped into the creek, it came to me that if he had a rifle, I was in the worst of all possible spots.

But he hadn't carried anything in his hands, and unless he'd hidden it above, say at the cabin, there wasn't anything to worry about.

I started up the trail, stopping every few feet to listen, but there was no sound except the birds in the woods above and the gentle gurgle of the water below.

I came to the trees and felt my eyes start to adjust as I entered the shade. The cabin was just ahead, and if he was there, he could probably hear my steps.

The hollow windows stared out at me, and I halted before the sagging porch.

There was no sound from within. I stepped onto the boards, tiptoed to the half-open door, and looked inside. Empty.

I returned the way I'd come, back down the trail to the creek and across. Whoever it was had vanished as suddenly as he had appeared. Whatever his business, it didn't seem that he had been a threat or would likely be one once our work got under way. A single, unarmed man generally wasn't dangerous to a crew of men with machetes.

The Blazer was just ahead, and I made a mental note to mention the incident to McNair when I got back to Jackson. But when I got to the vehicle and started to unlock the door, I realized it would be a lot longer than I'd planned before I could report the business to anybody.

While I'd been on the other side of the creek, following my will-o'-the-wisp, somebody else had cut both my front tires. I was just trying to decide what to do when I heard movement behind me and started to turn.

I didn't make it. Something clobbered me from behind, and the last thing I saw was the ground coming up in front of me.

# ≡ THREE

I came to sitting on the ground with my back against the Blazer's front fender, a sharp pain stabbing down through the top of my skull. When I felt my head, there was a lump like a goose egg but little blood. After a few deep breaths I muttered some choice words, staggered to my feet, and then reached into the glove compartment for my cell phone.

It was gone.

*Damn.*

I made some quick calculations. It was a mile back to the highway and after that three miles to town. I might get picked up on the blacktop, if there happened to be any traffic, but I hadn't seen much in my two trips up here. And whoever had done this might have gone that way, too. On the other hand, it was probably a quarter-mile from here to the cabin on the other side, and then, if McNair was right, another mile and a half to the Devlin place via the back pasture. The only other option was to head due west across the Buck Devlin place and come out on Highway 421 north of Cyn's house. But McNair had told me there were some pretty thick briar patches. Better to use the easier traverse of open pastures and rely on what charm I could muster if the owner saw me.

I got my machete out of the back of the Blazer, where it had been hidden with the rest of my tools, and took a Brunton compass for good measure. Then I headed back downhill and across the stream.

So had somebody followed me, or was it someone who was already here when I arrived? Could the mysterious man I'd seen headed for the cabin have doubled back? It seemed unlikely, but maybe he'd been working with a partner and had run away just to draw me off.

It seemed like a lot of trouble to go to.

I hurried up the slope, not stopping this time until I was in the cover of the trees. I rested for a few minutes, sitting on the porch of the cabin. My head still hurt, but I wasn't feeling any light-headedness or disorientation, so the blow probably hadn't done any serious damage. I heaved myself up and looked for the trail that would take me out.

It wasn't hard to find, but I took a compass bearing just in case. For twenty minutes I walked south through a pine forest smelling of ozone. Here and there I saw broken blades of grass, making me think my man had come this way a few minutes before, but it was hard to tell if the boot prints I saw in the dirt had been made that day or several days previously.

I checked my watch. It was eleven-thirty, and I was grateful for the shade. In another hour I'd have the full brunt of the June heat.

The trail wound right, and when I came out of the bend, I saw a gate ahead of me.

It was an iron frame, held in place by a rusty chain and a heavy Master padlock. A new-looking sign on the fence said:

*POSTED*
*TRESPASSERS WILL BE PROSECUTED*

Beyond the gate was an open pasture bordered by a fringe of hardwoods. Some cattle grazed nonchalantly on the sweet grass, and I saw stacks of hay piled on the other side of the field.

I took a deep breath and climbed over the fence.

The cattle raised their heads and watched. I looked for a bull but didn't see one. The path I was on was a pair of wheel ruts running alongside the fenceline. Across the fence I could see the land starting to drop off toward the creek. The sun was at its zenith now, pounding down like a big fist, and I wished I had a canteen. When I got to the other side of the field, I saw the trees ahead were just a windbreak and there was a cattle gap leading into another field on the other side. I rested in the shade for a few minutes, wondering if I'd made the right decision in coming this way. At least on the other route there was plenty of shade.

I crossed the cattle gap and started into the next field. There was some kind of shed in the distance but still no sign of the house. I checked my watch: five after noon. I couldn't have that much more to go.

I was halfway through the field when I saw the jeep.

It was headed straight for me along the ruts, and I knew they had seen me and it would do no good to try to duck over the fence or run.

There was nothing to do but stop and wait for them to reach me.

A second later I saw that there was only one person, the driver, and a few seconds after that I realized the driver was a woman.

*Cynthia Devlin . . .*

I stepped off the trail, and the jeep jerked to a halt a few feet from me. The driver wore jeans and a red shirt, and a bandanna covered her dark hair. I couldn't see her eyes because of the sunglasses, but there was no mistaking the displeasure in her face.

"You're probably wondering what I'm doing here," I said.

"You could say that," she replied. "There's a sign back there. This land is posted."

"I'm sorry," I said. "I had a kind of emergency, and this was the only route to take."

"What's that supposed to mean?" she asked, and for the first time I saw the carbine on the seat next to her. "How did you get back there in the first place if you didn't cross my land?"

"I came up Highway 952 on the East Feliciana side," I told her. "I was scouting the layout for some work I'm doing for the Corps of Engineers." I reached into my shirt pocket and handed her a business card. She regarded it skeptically.

"Moundmasters? What kind of name is that?"

"We're archaeologists. We're checking the project area for historic and prehistoric sites as part of the environmental impact statement."

"The Corps of Engineers doesn't own my land," she said.

"That's why I went on the other side, through the McNair tract. But somebody cut my tires and hit me on the head for my trouble. So I thought it would be easier if I came this way." I gave her my best smile. "I was hoping maybe you'd let me use your phone."

She stared at me for a long time.

"You've heard what I think of this project," she said.

"Yes, ma'am."

"You've got a lot of nerve." She jerked her head at the empty seat beside her. "Get in."

I climbed in, and she moved the gun so that it separated us like a bar.

"If they build this dam, won't they expropriate your land?" I asked.

"They'll try," she said. "But I'll slow 'em down, and maybe by then there'll be another governor and the dam won't seem like such a good idea."

"Did you grow up here?" I asked, trying to find common ground.

But she wasn't interested in talking. She just shook her head.

"No."

We came to the other side of the field, and I saw the house now through the trees. A red pickup with a camper sat in the yard behind it.

"By the way, I saw a man back there," I said. "He ran across the creek, headed in this direction. Did you see anybody else come through here?"

"Nobody came through here," she said and jerked the emergency brake. "Wait here. I have to go inside. Then I'll take you to town, and you can call a garage or whatever."

I watched her hop down, taking the rifle with her as if I might steal it. She headed for the back door, and as she opened it, a curtain moved in one of the back windows, and I realized someone was watching. I looked around the yard, tried to imagine soirees and lazy summer afternoons, but there was a tension that hung over the place. Partly it was the rigidity I sensed in the woman, but it also derived from what I'd heard about the deaths of her son and husband. This was an unhappy house, and Cynthia Devlin was, as I had been told, an angry woman.

She came back out a few minutes later and got back in without a word.

Ten minutes later we were in Jackson, and she turned off Highway 10, then slowed in front of the new red-brick post office.

"There's a phone in here," she said. "Next time, I'd appreciate it if you'd stay off my property."

I nodded. "I'll try to remember. And thank you."

I watched her make a U-turn and then disappear back the way we had come. I went into the post office, started to ask the woman at the counter where the police station was, and changed my mind. This had been outside the city, which made it sheriff's business. Instead, I found the pay phone and called the office to tell David I'd be late.

"Bombast called for you," he said. "She acted upset because you weren't here."

"Did she say what she wanted?" Maybe they were going to cancel the project. Good news for Cyn Devlin, but not very good news for our firm.

"She just wanted to tell you the delivery order is on its way."

"Thoughtful," I said.

I walked down to the Exxon station and asked if there was somebody who could drive me out to the McNair tract and bring a couple of tires in for repair. The owner gave me a funny look but called his mechanic.  Half an hour later we'd replaced one tire with the spare, pulled off the other front tire, and thrown both the ruined tires into the back of the pickup, leaving the Blazer's right front jacked up as we drove back to the gas station.

"I guess you figured there's people don't want this thing," the mechanic said. "But they don't got to cut people's tires."

"It could be worse," I said. "Didn't I hear about a man getting shot on that parcel last year?"

"Doug Devlin? Yeah. But that didn't have nothing to do with the dam. That was probably just a hunter shouldn't've been there."

We slowed as we came to Highway 10, and the driver jammed on the brakes. A red pickup with a camper flew past us, headed east, out of town, and I caught a glimpse of a man in a checked shirt behind the wheel.

It was the same truck I'd seen parked behind the Devlin house, and I was sure the driver was the mysterious man I'd followed up to the cabin. And yet she claimed she hadn't seen anyone . . .

"Have any idea who that was in the truck?" I asked.

The mechanic spit a stream of brown juice out his window.

"Looked like Blake Curtin. Probably been down there at Cyn's. Good pair," he grunted. "She's crazy and he don't talk."

"He's mute?"

"Like a possum, though they say he used to talk once."

"He's a friend of the family?" I asked.

"Friend of Doug's. Now he's friends with Cyn since Doug got killed." He spat again. "Does odd jobs, helps her keep the place up. Anyhow, that's what they say." He leered. "Well, it ain't none of my business."

We reached the filling station, and I waited while he pulled the old tires off the rims and replaced them with new ones. Then we drove back to the Blazer, and he put on one new tire and threw the other into the back. I followed him back to town and paid with my credit card, a hundred and ninety dollars when it was all done. Then I drove east through seven miles of rolling pasture lands to Clinton and parked on the square in front of the stately old white courthouse with columns and cupola. I went into the little steep-roofed brick building on the west side of the courthouse proper and presented myself to the bored deputy at the desk.

"I'd like to file a report," I said.

He listened to my complaint, told me I could have accomplished the same at the substation in Jackson, and then helped me fill out some papers.

"Don't expect much," he said. "Some folks just don't want that dam."

"They need to see their congressman, not me."

"Right."

"By the way, you know a man named Curtin?"

The deputy folded his arms.

"Blake Curtin?"

"That's right.

"You think he did this?"

"I don't know. I just saw him leaving the area in a hurry. He was headed for the Devlin place."

"I'm not surprised."

"He live around here?"

"On Highway 68, on the south side of Jackson. Has a trailer. But I wouldn't go trying to track down Blake. He ain't all there. I'd leave him to us."

"Whatever."

I drove back to Baton Rouge, gave my receipt to Marilyn, and gritted my teeth while she told me what that did to our cash flow.

"We'll find some way to charge it off to the project," I said lamely.

That night I fed Digger, my mixed shepherd, and took him for a walk. He seemed to know my mood, and his ears drooped slightly, as if in sympathy. Afterward I sat alone in the old house on Park Boulevard and listened to the ghosts come and go. The ghosts spoke as creaks and groans and the scraping of branches against the eaves. Sometimes I imagined that I heard the voices of my parents. And other times I thought I heard Pepper's voice calling to me from upstairs, where I slept.

Sometimes I was angry with her for leaving, but then I told myself that I was reading too much into it, that she'd be back.

But why leave in the first place? I'd offered her a place in the firm.

And maybe that was the problem: She didn't want to accept anything she didn't feel she'd earned. So she'd taken time off to think it over.

Ghosts.

I found myself wondering if Cyn Devlin had ghosts in her husband's house, too.

Then I thought about the lonely little cabin. Why was it linked to Oswald? Had someone actually seen him there in 1963, during his brief trip to the Felicianas? Or were there things about his trip that no one had ever found out?

Ghosts . . . maybe that was what it was all about, anyway, because this whole part of the world was filled with them. The ghosts of the early settlers, like Bernardo de Galvez, the Spanish governor who had named the Felicianas after his wife; the ghost of Huey Long, who had been shot by a mild-mannered doctor and now stood in the capitol gardens encased in bronze; the ghosts of my parents, who still haunted the old family home on Park Boulevard . . .

That night I dreamed I was standing by the creek with the land reaching up on either side of me. As I started across the sandbar, I heard a roaring, and when I looked up, I saw a wall of water rushing toward me. I turned to run, but it caught me in midstride and sucked me into its depths. Around me I saw bits of trees and stones, and I knew that I was dying.

It was just before darkness closed over me that I saw him, a slightly built young man with a sneer, rifle clutched in his right hand, a holster around his waist. He was turning over and over, and I wondered how he managed to keep from thrashing.

Then I realized where I had seen him before. It was in a photograph we'd all seen: Lee Harvey Oswald, standing in his backyard, with his rifle. Lee, the assassin . . .

# FOUR

The next morning we interviewed potential crew for the dam project. There were four applicants, two men and two women. One of the men was a business major and his skin was the color of dead fish. He'd be a candidate for heat stroke, and I told David to hire the other three.

"What about the Lawrence girl," he asked. "You think she can cut it?"

One of the female applicants was a thick-bodied Cajun who looked like she could wrestle a bear. The Lawrence girl, however, was petite, with black hair in a page-boy cut and a vivacious smile.

I reread her application.

Meg Lawrence. Third year anthropology student. Summer field school last year. Two courses in geology.

"I don't see anything wrong," I said.

He shrugged. "I know this sounds funny, but there was something about her smile."

"Her *smile?*"

"I have a gut feeling she may be trouble."

I scanned the references on her vitae. One of them was from Stuart Laskar, an archaeologist at the University.

"I'll check her out," I said. "But unless there's some horror story . . ."

David nodded, and I put the applications aside.

I suddenly realized I hadn't eaten and walked over to Louie's for *huevos rancheros* and a cup of iced coffee.

When I got back, I was still fidgety. I didn't think Blake

Curtin had cut my tires yesterday and jumped me, but why had he acted so suspiciously, and why had the Devlin woman lied about seeing him? I was a stranger, so why did it matter what I thought? I had the sense of plunging into something more than a mere archaeological survey, and I didn't like the feeling. Then I remembered what Clyde Fontenot had told me: Cyn's brother-in-law, Buck, lived in Baton Rouge. All at once I wanted to know what he could tell me about the land and about his sister-in-law, her strange friend, and the way her husband had died.

There were only two Devlins in the phone book, one a married couple and the other a Francis. I tried the second and waited while the phone rang. On the fifth buzz, as I was about to hang up, a man's voice answered.

"Is this Buck Devlin?" I asked.

"That's right. Who is this?"

I told him my name. "I'm under contract to the Corps of Engineers to do part of the environmental impact statement for the property you own near Jackson. I wonder if I could come talk to you about it?"

"Now?"

"Is that possible?"

"Why the hell not?"

"I'll be over in ten minutes," I said.

His house was a white frame structure on Arrowhead, just off Lee. The lawn was neatly trimmed, and there was a rock-bordered garden with jonquils and dahlias. A Bronco sat in the driveway, its front facing the street as if liable to be called upon for a getaway.

I rang the bell and waited, but after a minute there was no response, so I walked around to the driveway and made my way to the backyard.

What caught my eye first was the deck with what appeared to be a hot tub. Then I saw the man.

Buck Devlin was stripped to the waist, crouching over a set of barbells. Though he was ten years my senior, his muscles rippled as he lifted the bar to his chest and began a series of presses. Sweat rolled down his torso, and his neck muscles bulged. The bandanna that held his hair out of his face was soaked through. As he lifted, he counted silently, and I sensed he still didn't know I was there. When he was finished, he eased the barbell to the ground, threw back his head, and gulped in the air.

"Mr. Devlin," I said.

His head came around slowly to fix on me.

"That's me," he said, reaching for a towel.

"I'm sorry to break in," I said. "I'll try not to take too much of your time."

"Too much of my time." Devlin smiled and nodded and finished drying himself with his towel. The back door of the house opened, and an oriental woman looked out and asked a question in a language I couldn't understand. Devlin answered back and then came over with his hand outstretched.

"She asked if you wanted any iced tea. I told her I didn't know but bring an extra glass. She's a good woman. Her father did the garden. You like it?"

"Very beautiful," I said.

The woman appeared with a tray holding a pitcher and two glasses. She set it on the deck and disappeared back into the house. She was not much more than twenty, with a tiny waist and a round face.

"I managed to get her and her parents over here," Devlin said, pouring tea into a glass and handing it to me. "A connection in State."

"You were in the Army," I said.

He nodded. "But not much of what I did in the last ten years was what people think of as military."

For the first time I noticed the eagle tattoo on his right shoulder.

"I hear you're in favor of expropriating your sister-in-law's property near Jackson."

"That's right. It isn't really her property. Not in the moral sense. She never did a damned thing to earn it. It was in our family long before she ever met Doug."

"You don't like her," I said.

"No. I told him she was a gold digger when he met her, and I haven't changed my mind. She came from north Louisiana trailer trash. When she found Doug, she dug in her hooks like an assassin bug, and she hasn't let go yet."

"Why do you think she's against this dam?"

"Because if they build it, she'll have a recreational lake in her backyard with people fishing and waterskiing. Maybe there're things she doesn't want 'em to see."

"But you think the dam is a good idea."

"It'll make money for me. That's all I care about." He sipped his tea and then put the glass down on the tray.

"Look, Graham, I was in the Army for thirty-six years. I went places nobody in their right mind would go." He pointed to a scarred area on his stomach. "You see that? I got ripped open by a sharp piece of bamboo held by somebody who thought I knew something. I retired as a lieutenant colonel, and they gave me the National Security Medal. You know what kind of pension that is? I never lived on that damn land. If somebody wants to buy it, that's fine with me. If Doug was living, I might hold off if he had strong feelings. But not for Cyn. She doesn't have any claim."

"What about a man named Blake Curtin?" I asked. "You ever heard of him?"

The colonel's gray eyes narrowed. "What did you hear about Curtin?"

I shrugged. "I was there yesterday and saw him at the place. He seems to hang around, and I was wondering if he'll be a problem."

"Screw him. If he gives you any trouble, call the sheriff and have his butt thrown in jail. He's just like Cyn—they're two of a kind. He was Doug's friend, you know."

I finished my tea.

"You ever been to that cabin on your land?" I asked.

"Sure. I expect they'll tear it down. Nobody's used it for twenty years."

"Not Lee Oswald's ghost?" I said.

Devlin frowned slightly, then threw back his head and laughed, but I thought the laugh was forced.

"You've heard the stories, eh?"

"Just thought I'd ask."

"You know, I was home from boot camp that summer before Kennedy was shot. I don't remember anything about Oswald being there. I think it's something they made up to put the place on the map. Every other town in Louisiana's got Lafitte's treasure. Jackson's got Kennedy's assassin.''

"You're probably right," I allowed. "And I don't guess there's anything else on that land—like an Indian site?"

"Not that I know of. But you're free to look." He got up and stuck out a hand. "Well, good luck, or, as we used to say, good hunting. And don't let Cyn run you off."

"Thank you, Colonel."

That afternoon I called Stuart Laskar at the anthropology department and asked him about Meg Lawrence. When he chuckled, I got an uneasy feeling.

"Does that mean she's trouble?"

"No. She did well at our field school last year. Carried her load and then some. Polite, bright, good personality."

"But?"

"Nothing. I recommend her."

"Then why is David doubtful?"

Stuart chuckled again. "Meg makes some people uneasy. She says what's on her mind. Some people can't deal with that."

I thought over what he had said, then called Meg Lawrence and told her to report in field gear the next morning.

When I hung up, I told David I was going to the map library in the geography department to review some aerial photos. We had a little waste dump project of a hundred acres near Carencro, and I wanted to make sure there were no structures shown in the Soil Conservation Service photos taken in the early forties. But in reality I wanted to drop by the history department and talk to Byron Foster. Byron was a specialist in recent American history. He'd never risen above associate professor because he spent most of his time with his students instead of grinding out publications, and I found him in his office now with a student while another waited her turn in the hall. I went to the library, which is only a few steps away, located the volume I was looking for, and when I came back, Byron was free.

"So what've you got there?" he asked, smiling through his gray beard. "A list of all the aboriginal pottery types in the Mississippi Valley?"

"No, something more in your line," I said and laid my book on the desk for him to see.

He twisted his head to look at it and then whistled.

"The Warren Report? Don't tell me they asked you to evaluate the Texas Book Depository for the National Register."

"Not quite." I told him about the project, my meeting with Cyn Devlin, and, finally, the rumors of Oswald's visit. "Anything to that, do you know?"

Byron shrugged his big shoulders, a bear confined to a chair.

"If there is, it isn't in *there*. I taught a seminar on the Kennedy presidency a few years ago, and I had to bone up on the assassination. So far as I know, Oswald went from Dallas to New Orleans in 1963 and then back to Texas. Not that he *couldn't've* gotten up to Jackson or Clinton while he was in New Orleans that summer, but one thing you have to keep in mind—he couldn't drive."

"What about some of his New Orleans friends? Couldn't they have taken him?"

"Maybe. But there's no good evidence he *had* any friends in New Orleans. Or any place, for that matter. I don't care what the film said, or what Jim Garrison claimed. You and I both know that evidence Garrison dug up for the Shaw trial was a bunch of crap. And the jury knew it, too. Oswald was, as the Warren Commission wrote, a very alienated person."

"No conspiracy, no plot?"

"What's a conspiracy? So Oswald's with some other kooks in New Orleans and somebody says, 'They ought to shoot Kennedy.' Oswald remembers and carries it out. Is that a conspiracy?" He reached for his pipe and started to fill it. "Remember, Oswald had already tried to kill General Walker in April. Whatever he heard, whatever influences there were, he was, to all intents and purposes, playing a lone hand. Or is that something you didn't want to hear?"

"No, I can accept it."

The historian lit his pipe, and a few seconds later the room was filled with sweet smoke.

"I remember that Friday. I was in my senior year at

Tulane. I was standing in line at the Union for lunch. Somebody said, 'The president's been shot in Dallas.' I turned around and almost spilled somebody's tray. I saw people all over the room with their heads together, funny looks on their faces. I left the chow line and went to find a TV set. I never did eat that day.''

Smoke floated up to the ceiling in silence and crawled along the acoustic tiles.

"What happened to us that day?" he whispered. "Was that when everything started to come apart? Vietnam, Watergate, the Iran hostages . . ." He shook his head. "We talked about it in the seminar. How there were other events. The U-2 incident, for example. Before that, nobody even thought to question the government when it put out a story. Or the Bay of Pigs and the way Kennedy left the invaders stranded on that beach. The missile crisis . . . But that day in Dallas—it was so damned impossible.''

I didn't say anything, but even though I'd only been in the fourth grade when Kennedy died, I'd felt some of the same things.

"Alan, it sounds more like it's in the domain of the folklore people. But let me know what you find out.''

I got up to go, but his hand caught my arm.

"Look, I'm having some folks over tomorrow night. Plan to come.''

I nodded. "Thanks. What can I bring?''

"Pepper, if she can come.''

"She's in Mexico. A dig," I said, a pang shooting through me at the sound of her name.

Byron studied me for a moment like an owl and then smiled.

"I'll try to fix you up then.''

I said goodbye and walked out with the Warren Report. He was probably right about Oswald. But the rumors had whetted my curiosity. Maybe, after I'd written Pepper a long letter tonight, I'd do some reading.

# ■ FIVE

The waste dump job was a version of hell. A recent rain had made a mire out of the survey area, a series of plowed fields. The mud sucked at our boots, and when we stopped, we sank further into the gumbo. The sun had reached its full summer fury, and a steamy mist hugged the ground, plastering our clothes to our bodies. We finished the job at four, more dead than alive, and slogged our way back to the Blazer. Sum total: no artifacts, no sites.

"Well, how did you like it?" I asked one of the new people, Chris Keller.

He shook his head. "Are all the jobs like this?"

"Only the easy ones," David said, and Chris's mouth dropped open. Meg smiled.

"When's the next one?" she asked.

That evening I relaxed in the old four-footed bathtub, letting the water eat away the smell of the field. I knew why Meg was trouble now: Nobody else on the crew could keep up with her. A sure way to upset the men. Well, that was their problem. I closed my eyes and reached for my beer.

What was Pepper doing right now? Was she still grimy from her day in the field? The rainy season was about to begin, so they were probably racing to finish up on site before heading for the lab in Chetumal. Or were they already in the lab? Lounging on the beach with Cubas in their hands, while a suave Eric Blackburn, wife and family far away, regaled her with exaggerations from a career fueled by his family's money and old boy connections?

The phone started to ring, and I jumped up, splashing water on the floor. Maybe it was her.

By the time I got to the phone, it had stopped ringing, and the message light of the answering machine was on.

I pressed the Playback button and died a little when I heard her voice.

"Hi, Alan, I just wanted to call. We're leaving to head down to Belize. There's a man I need to talk to about some colonial documents. I'll try to call when I find out where we're staying. I—" I heard a man's voice in the background, too distant to make out. "Well, take care."

The line went dead.

I dialed the number she'd left for me, and after a series of clicks as it made the international connection, the phone started to ring. But I was too late: They were already gone.

*Damn.*

I wandered back to the bathroom and finished drying myself. As I did, I looked at my face in the mirror. A little blurry without my glasses, the brown hair not as thick as a few years back, but not a bad face. I liked to think it showed what my mother called character. Not pretty-boy handsome, like Eric Blackburn's face. You didn't get character by sliding upward through life.

Pepper would never be deceived by mere looks and money.

Would she?

I shaved, donned a fresh guayabera, a pair of clean khaki pants, and Mexican sandals. Then I picked up a six-pack of Dos Equis at a convenience store and drove over to Foster's place.

Byron lived on West Parker, just outside the south gates of the campus. It was a shady neighborhood of sleepy old houses mixed in with newer apartment complexes, catering to students and younger faculty.

His own house, which he'd bought ten years before, was a low wood-frame with azaleas in the front and a trellis with honeysuckle. There were cars already there, and I heard soft rock music. I could never keep Byron's love life straight: Sometimes there was a young woman, and other times he lived alone. This time I was met by a blonde in her thirties, who identified herself as Clea and acted as if she was organizing the affair. The other guests were a mixture of graduate students and faculty, and I exchanged greetings with the people I knew.

I was escorted past a center table, with chips and dips, and another table against the wall, with an assortment of liquors. Byron was in the kitchen, talking to a woman whose long, dark hair cascaded down her back.

"Ah, Alan." He disengaged as he saw me. "I'm glad you could make it. I want you to meet somebody."

He touched the woman lightly on the arm, and she turned around. Even as her expression showed her surprise, I realized I'd seen her before.

"This is one of my students, Cyn Devlin. Cyn, this is Alan Graham."

"We've met," I stammered, trying to convince myself that the woman in front of me was the same one who had all but run me off her land.

"Oh, really?" Byron asked. "Well, then I can leave you two alone and say hello to some of my other guests." And he was gone, leaving us staring at each other.

"I didn't know you were going to be here," she managed.

"I didn't know you were a friend of Byron's," I responded.

"Why, am I too old to be a student?"

"Of course not. Look, I didn't come here to fight."

"Me either. Maybe I came across too strong the other day, but you can't know what it's like to have people crawling all over your land."

"I try not to crawl," I said.

"A bad choice of words."

"Well, maybe not. Sometimes I feel like I'm crawling."

She gave me a tiny smile, and I noticed for the first time that she was really a beautiful woman, with a pointed chin and creamy skin.

"Can I get you something to drink?" I asked.

She motioned to a glass on the counter. "I have some Coke."

"Nothing stronger?"

"No."

I opened one of my beers and put the rest in the refrigerator.

"So will you shoot me if I use the trail to the cabin to get back to Buck's property?"

"Probably not." She gave a hopeless little shrug. "There'll be enough people back there, anyway."

"If it ever gets off the ground," I said. "Lots of these projects never get built."

"And lots of them *do*."

"Maybe we should start over," I said. "Tell me what you're studying."

"History," she said. "I'm a junior. I need twenty-eight more hours to graduate. I figure I can do it in two semesters, three if I go part-time." She picked up her glass. "I intend to be halfway educated before I die."

"You're not from around here," I said.

"No. I'm from Farmerville, in Union Parish. My father grew beans until he drank his way out of the land. Then he went to Monroe and became a construction laborer until he dropped a block of cement on his foot. Good excuse to drink some more. There were six of us, and I left home when I was fifteen, married when I was sixteen."

"Mr. Devlin?"

She gave a bitter little chuckle. "Doug didn't come along until a lot later. No, Number one was a drummer in a band. Died of an overdose when he was twenty-six. I didn't meet Doug until I was an ancient twenty." She poured herself some more Coke. "He figured he could make an honest woman out of me. It cost him the goodwill of most of his family."

The sarcasm in her tone was unmistakable.

"And did he make an honest woman out of you?"

She nodded and then looked me in the eyes. "Yes. At least, until our son died." She looked away. "So why isn't an archaeologist teaching at the university?"

"I did once," I told her. "My teaching methods were too unorthodox, and I was having a hard time with a relationship. Things kind of fell apart for a little while."

"And you came here?"

"I grew up here. My father was old and sick, and I came home to be with him. Then he died, and I wasn't sure what I was going to do. But I ran into my old anthropology professor, Sam MacGregor, one day and he said he needed some help on a job he was doing. He'd just retired and was doing a lot of consulting in contract archaeology. We set up a company together, and then a few years later he retired again and left me with his clientele. I've been running it ever since."

"You didn't marry?"

"A long time ago. It didn't work."

"And there's nobody now?"

"There is. But she's in Mexico."

"What do you do in the meantime? Besides archaeology, I mean."

"I have a collection of fifties rock records, the Platters, Fats Domino, some Jerry Lee Lewis. I like to listen to them and I like old movies on the VCR. I play poker with my friends when their wives let them, and I like to cook."

"And you like parties, I guess."

"I don't really go to that many."

She stared at me and didn't say anything.

"I guess some day when I'm too old for it, I'll get out of the game," I said. "But nobody's ever retired from contract archaeology."

"Why not?"

"It's too new. Part of the environmental movement."

"And yet you're helping them build that thing."

"I'm just doing a survey."

"Yes."

Suddenly I felt like a Nazi.

"We've found some necessary sites that way," I explained. "Sites that would have gone unreported without us."

For some reason it was necessary that I make her understand.

"Would you like to see our lab?" I asked.

She hesitated and then shrugged. "Sure. When?"

"How about now?"

"Now?"

"It's just the other side of the campus."

She stared back at me, then put down her glass.

"All right."

We slipped out without anyone noticing, and I led her to the Blazer. I drove up Highland and out the north gates to State Street, where I turned right. I went south on Carlotta and a few seconds later was stopping before the old house where we worked.

"Not the best neighborhood," I said, "but low rent goes with archaeology."

I showed her up the walk, opened the door, and punched the code into the alarm pad. Then I turned on the lights.

The vessel our student had been working on was now completely reconstructed, and I lifted it off the table for Cyn to examine.

"You see the curving lines? Marksville motif: This bowl is two thousand years old. We found it in a site in Pointe Coupée Parish. We think the people that made it had some kind of trade connections with the mound builders of the Ohio Valley."

"Do you do radiocarbon dating here?" she asked.

"No, that requires a special lab and a few million dollars' worth of equipment. Even the university here doesn't have a radiocarbon lab. We have to send our samples off."

On one of the other tables was a fragment of flintlock rifle.

"Eighteenth century," I explained. "Probably English."

She lifted it, turned it over in the light, and then put it back down.

"Looks to be about fifty caliber," she said.

"You know about guns?"

"My husband was a gun collector. I picked up some of it from him."

"Was he hunting when he was killed?" I asked.

"No. I'm not sure just what he was doing. All I know is it had something to do with the cabin."

"The cabin?"

She looked away, and when she spoke again, her voice was flat.

"There were these rumors—you've probably heard

them—about Lee Oswald's ghost hanging around there. None of us believed that, except that after our boy died, I started to get the feeling somebody was using the cabin for something. I told Doug, but he never saw anybody. It was just footprints and cigarette butts. I told him it was probably some poacher or maybe kids were sneaking back there, but he said it was something else and he was going to find out. So he left early one morning and went back to wait. I didn't like the idea, and I even wanted to go with him, but he had his rifle and he could handle himself.''

I waited, afraid of what she was about to say.

"When he didn't come back by noon, I went looking for him."

"Look, if you don't want to talk about it . . ."

"I saw where he'd been at the cabin: His blanket was still there. I followed the trail to the end of the woods and looked down at the creek, and that was when I saw him. He was lying just on the other side, facedown, with his rifle next to him. I knew he was dead, but I went down and looked anyway.''

She was staring into the past now, and I was no longer in the room.

"There was a wound in his head, and I knew he'd been shot. Somebody with a military rifle, an old 6.5 millimeter, the State Police laboratory said.'' She turned her face toward me until she was staring up into my eyes. "Don't you see? A 6.5, the kind a Mannlicher-Carcano fires.''

"A Mannlicher-Carcano?''

She nodded. "Yes. The kind of weapon Oswald used to kill President Kennedy.''

SIX

"It has to be a coincidence," I said.

"That's what the investigators said. It was a screwed-up investigation because he was found across the creek, in East Feliciana, but the shot may have come from West Feliciana. Nobody could decide who was supposed to run the thing. It ended up with the two sheriffs at each other's throats, and, of course, that started the rumor that there was a cover-up. Now there are people in the area who're sure it has something to do with the Kennedy assassination."

I shrugged. "There have to be lots of Mannlicher-Carcanos around. They were selling them for twenty-five bucks back when Oswald bought his. It could have come from anywhere."

"I know where it came from," she said.

It was my second surprise.

"Just before Doug was killed, the house was burglarized. Some of Doug's guns were stolen. One of them was a Mannlicher-Carcano."

"Was there all this Oswald talk before that happened?"

"I've thought about that, too. It seems to me there was talk about Oswald coming to Jackson to apply for work at the hospital, but there wasn't anything connecting him with the cabin. I think it all came about because of the kind of gun that was stolen and somebody in town added two and two and got five."

I walked over to the bulletin board and my eyes wandered up to a notice the government had sent us saying no

41

employee could be forced to take a polygraph.

"Tell me about Blake Curtin," I said, turning around and leaning back against the wall.

Her face went expressionless. "What about him?"

"He was at the house when you took me there. He was the man I saw down at the creek. Why did you lie about him?"

Her eyes narrowed and I saw her stiffen.

"I think," she said, "you'd better take me back."

As I slowed in front of Byron's house, she was already opening the door and was out of the Blazer before I could pull in at the curb. I sat for a moment with my motor idling and then drove back to the office. I got out the topographic map and the big aerial photo the Corps had sent me and studied them. I didn't know what I was looking for, and nothing jumped out at me. Finally I put them aside and went home.

The next morning, Saturday, I drove up to Jackson, parked in front of the post office, and went in. The barbershop was probably a better place to get information, but there were too many ears there. I was hoping I could find Adolph Dewey and that he'd be alone. I was in luck.

"Can I help you?" he asked from behind the counter, a visor shading his face.

I told him who I was and he nodded.

"I remember. You went off with Clyde. Well, did he confuse you enough?"

He was sixtyish, with gray, western-style sideburns and a thick mop of gray hair poking over the green eyeshade.

"No, but I'm pretty confused anyway. I thought maybe you could help."

Dewey nodded. "If I can."

"The land that used to belong to Sam Pardue on the East Feliciana side: I understand it's leased to a hunting club."

"Two Parish Club it's called. Why?"

"Know who belongs?"

"I reckon so. I'm the secretary."

"Could I get a list of the members?"

"Ain't no secret. There's me, there's Gus Winchell, the barber, that you met; there's Gene McNair—he's the president—and there's Doc Childe from the hospital. Oh, and five or six from over near Clinton. Why?''

"What about Clyde Fontenot?"

"Clyde don't hunt." The postmaster smiled. "He wouldn't know which way to point the gun."

"I see. Of course, you'll be losing the hunting club if this dam goes through."

Dewey shrugged. "Can't do nothing about that. Why? Is somebody in the club giving you a hard time?"

I told him about my cut tires and bump on the head.

"I doubt that was our folks. We're sportsmen, not poachers. Now, if I was you, I'd be looking at somebody who had no business being there. Somebody with a ax to grind."

"Any names come to mind?"

"Can't say." His eyes narrowed slightly. "But Sam Pardue's always felt like that land was his. We had a deal with him when he owned it, see: He could still hunt it without paying club dues. When he sold it, we agreed to keep him in, like before. But when he found out they planned to develop it, he kind of went off his rocker. Said he hadn't sold the land for no dam and the McNairs had taken advantage of him. He was hot as hell. I'm not saying he did anything more'n talk, now, but I'm saying that might be where you oughta look."

"Where does he live?" I asked.

"Sam? Over the other side of Clinton on Highway 67."

I wrote down the directions and thanked him.

"By the way, you hear about this Lee Harvey Oswald business?" I asked.

He nodded. "I heard about it."

"Got an opinion?"

He set down his pencil and rested both hands on the countertop.

"I only know he was here."

"You know it?"

The postmaster nodded. "That's right. I saw him with my own eyes."

He stared at me as if daring me to say he was wrong.

"You saw Lee Oswald here in Jackson," I said.

"No, it wasn't here, it was in Clinton. Late August,

1963. They were having some kind of voter registration drive for the niggers. I was a deputy sheriff then and I was in the old sheriff's office in the courthouse. He come up to me and asked me where he was supposed to go to register to vote."

"To vote?"

"That's right. He was looking for work, and somebody told him he might be able to get on at the state hospital, but he'd do better if he was a registered voter in the parish."

"He told you his name?"

"Yeah. I remember saying it was a name they didn't have around here and where was he from, and he said New Orleans. Afterward I went out to see how the voter thing was going and I seen him get into this big Caddie with a white-haired fellow driving."

"And you recognized him later, after the assassination?"

"After I heard the name of the assassin. That's when I remembered. I looked at the pictures, and it was the same man. There're others who saw him here, though. I'm not the only one."

"You've heard about the stories that he went to the cabin on the Devlin place?"

Dewey snorted. "That's just kids. I don't believe none of that. I think the man went to the hospital and applied and they turned him down and that was the end of that. But that don't make as good a story as saying he went to this cabin and hid out."

"I guess you told your story to the investigators."

The postmaster shook his head. "Warren Commission never sent nobody to talk to us. Wasn't 'til Garrison started his thing in New Orleans anybody listened to what we had to say. I testified at the Shaw trial. Didn't do no good."

"You think Clay Shaw was the man driving Oswald around that day?"

"Can't say for sure. Some said it was."

I started away, then stopped. "I understand that Doug Devlin was killed with the same kind of gun that killed Kennedy."

Dewey nodded. "I hear tell. Can't matter, though."

"Oh?"

"Oswald's dead. Jack Ruby shot him in Dallas. Dead man can't kill nobody with *no* kind of rifle. Now can he?"

It was hard to argue with that kind of logic.

The Pardue house was a brick, ranch-style structure with a wooden wagon wheel on the front lawn. The grass was well trimmed, and there was a sign over the door that said, *Sam and Angie*. A pickup truck was in the drive, and as I got out, a collie came bounding up to greet me. I heard hammering from the back and let the dog lead me around the side of the house. A huge pecan tree shaded most of the backyard, and there was a ladder leading up to one of the branches. At the top of the ladder was a wood structure, and as I approached, I saw a man halfway up the ladder, hard at work, while a woman held it steady from below.

She turned as I approached.

"Sam," she said.

The man at the top of the ladder looked around and laid aside his hammer.

I told them my name, and Sam Pardue started down the ladder, moving a few inches at a time, as if the whole business might fall on top of him if he wasn't careful. When he got to the bottom, I saw that he'd been a big man in his prime. But now he seemed hollowed out, his cheeks stretched taut over the bones and his eyes sunk into his head. His wife moved toward him protectively.

"Trying to build the grandchildren a tree house," he said, panting. "Been promising for a couple of years now. Finally decided I better do it now if it was gonna get done."

I told him my business. "I was wondering if you knew of any Indian sites or anything else of historical value on the property you sold to Mr. McNair."

Sam Pardue stared at me for a second, sucking in his cheeks. His shoulders were rounded, and he hunched over like his bones had melted.

"Did he tell you to come here?"

"No," I said.

Pardue nodded.

"The whole damned bunch of 'em are crooks. They stole

my land. Knew I was sick, that I needed money for the radiation treatments. Sent that Gene McNair up talking so sweet you'd of thought he was sucking honey. Said he'd buy it and keep it as a hunting club. Two months after I sold it, I heard they were going to sell it to the state for ten times what they paid me." He broke into a fit of coughing, and his wife clutched his arm. "Now I'm running out of money for my treatments. I had to sell off part of the back forty."

"I'm sorry."

"All I want to do is finish this tree house. I promised the grandkids. I promised I'd get it done before I go."

"You aren't going anywhere yet," his wife said, but from the pallor in his face I could see the truth, and it was clear that he knew it.

"Do you remember when Mrs. Devlin's husband got killed?" I asked. "I think he was found on your land."

The old man gave me a level stare. "I remember."

"Do you think it was a hunting accident?"

"No. It was August. That isn't deer season."

"Any ideas on who might have done it?"

He rubbed his nose and turned around.

"Ask the sheriff. Now I got to get back to my tree house."

I saw that I wasn't going to make any headway, so I turned around and left. But one thing was clear: Sam Pardue knew something. And he didn't want to say what.

# ■ SEVEN

I drove back to Jackson, noting that the pasture land on both sides of the road was given to stock raising rather than farming. The soil was too poor to allow profitable agriculture. I was thinking about Cynthia Devlin and her big house and wondering how she managed to survive. The cattle I'd seen were Herefords, not Brahmas, and there weren't that many of them. Maybe there had been more cattle while her husband was alive and she'd had to sell them. There were questions I needed answered, and I could only think of one person to answer them and that was Clyde Fontenot.

His wife told me he was out back and then went inside quickly, as if she didn't want to be involved. I walked around the house to the garden, all roses and lilies fringed by elephant grass, and looked for Clyde. There was a tool-shed at the rear behind the birdbath, and after a minute I heard something inside, like the clash of metal. I went along the path, stepping from one flagstone to another, and saw Clyde inside, bent over something that I at first took to be a lawn mower.

"Mr. Fontenot," I said.

His head jerked up, and for a second I thought his glasses would fall off. Then he straightened them with both hands and smiled.

"Dr. Graham. What brings you up here?"

I saw that what he was working on wasn't a lawn mower, but a wooden pole with some kind of disk on the end and

47

wires going to a box on the floor. He thrust the contraption to the side and turned his body so that he blocked my view of his project.

"I used to be a science teacher," he said. "I'm sort of an inventor, you might say."

"Maybe you could invent a lie detector to tell me when folks around here are telling me the truth," I said.

He squinted at me, and then his face cracked into a smile.

"Getting a runaround, are you? Who is it, Cyn?"

"Partly. Nobody seems to want to say just why her husband got killed. Sam Pardue sounds like he knows, but he won't tell. Cyn says he was stalking a poacher, but *why* isn't clear. I mean what would a poacher be doing on that land? Then there's the land itself: I didn't see a big agricultural operation. The tree growth is fifty years old, so nobody's made any money logging anytime lately. And the cattle aren't a prize herd. The place needs work, but there's a man who hangs around—this Blake Curtin. When I parked on the McNair tract, somebody cut my tires and slugged me from behind, but it's Curtin who ran away. In the sheriff's office they don't seem to know anything. So I thought I'd come to the town historian and ask if you know what the hell's going on."

The little man cackled.

"Getting the treatment, eh?"

"You could say that. And I don't feel comfortable putting a crew out in a place where there are things happening that I don't understand."

Fontenot straightened up the rest of the way and wiped his hand on a rag. I glimpsed a car battery and a tangle of wire on the cement floor by his feet.

"What else have you heard?"

"I heard that Lee Oswald haunts that cabin on Buck Devlin's place."

Clyde exhaled like a leaking tire, then stooped down, picked up a screwdriver, and put it on the shelf.

"And you don't believe it."

"Oswald's been buried for thirty-six years."

"Buried," Fontenot repeated. "But that doesn't mean he's really dead."

"Pardon?"

"The kids around here claim to see him. I heard it all the time when I was teaching. It was a story long before Doug Devlin got killed. The kids used to come in and tell me about it: A slight, young-looking man walking through the woods or along the creek. Sometimes in broad daylight. One of the boys asked him what he was doing, and the man said he was looking for something. But more often it's at night. They see his face in the window, or they hear his voice."

"I'm sure it makes a good story."

"Sure does. Now let me ask you something, Dr. Graham: I want you to try to put yourself in somebody's place, all right?"

"Sure. Whose?"

"Well, try to imagine you're young, you're unhappy, you're out of work, and your marriage is in bad shape. You run into some people who say they can help you—older men, men that seem totally in control, who seem to care what happens to you, to value what you have to say. Men who want to help you."

"All right." I wasn't sure where he was going.

"Then suppose they get you a job. All they ask is that on a certain day you do them a favor: You don't show up for work. So you stay home and then you hear a horrible thing's happened: Somebody's killed the president of the United States, and it seems like the shots came from where you work, the sixth floor of the building. You hear the police are looking for you, so you leave your house and hide in a movie theater. But they find you and drag you out. You swear you're innocent, but they parade you in front of the cameras. Then, two days later, while they're moving you somewhere else, a man steps out of the crowd and shoots you."

"Then you're dead," I said.

He brought his face close to my own, and I smelled coffee on his breath.

"Do you believe in life after death, Dr. Graham?"

"I think it's possible."

"Then isn't it also possible that this man, who has been

set up, framed by people he thought were his friends, accused of a terrible crime, and then assassinated himself—isn't it just possible his essence, or personality, or psyche, as the Greeks called it, might return to a place that he associates with a turning point in his life on earth?"

"Yes," I said again, "it's possible."

I didn't add that I also considered it possible that the sun wouldn't rise in the morning.

"So now maybe you understand better."

I remembered Dewey the assistant postmaster asking if Clyde had managed to confuse me. I saw what he meant now.

"You're saying, among other things, that there was a conspiracy to kill Kennedy and that Oswald wasn't involved except as a dupe."

Fontenot nodded slowly, his eyes hard on mine. I looked for the kind of glaze that indicated madness, but, oddly, I didn't see what I expected.

"That's right. I'm saying that the brains behind the Kennedy murder was somebody else."

"Clay Shaw?"

Fontenot shook his head. "Shaw was an underling."

"Then who?"

The little man gave me a sideways glance. "Not who. *How many.*"

"Senator Buell McNair? He was younger then than I am."

"Young but on his way to power."

"Old Timothy Devlin?"

Fontenot smiled. "Timothy hated the Kennedys. He was a states' rights man."

"Who else?"

"I didn't say anybody. I'm not a fool. Some of 'em are still alive."

"They killed Douglas Devlin?"

Fontenot shrugged. "He was too close maybe."

"What was his financial situation? Did he have a successful farm?"

"Now you're close, too."

"You're saying it was blackmail? That Doug Devlin was

blackmailing the conspirators to make up for losses?''

"I'm not saying anything. It's too dangerous.''

"And Doug's brother, Buck?''

"How do you know that's really Buck? When was the last time anybody around here saw Buck? How do we know who sent him?''

"Then what does the dam project have to do with it all?''

Fontenot licked his lips.

"The land will be flooded. The cabin will be taken down.''

"And?''

"The spirit will have nowhere to go. Don't you see?'' He leaned close to me then. "The only one who can bring it all to light is the ghost: Lee Oswald's spirit. They have to destroy that. *They* have to kill Lee Oswald again!''

# ■ EIGHT

When I got back to the office, there was a message on the answering machine from Meg Lawrence asking me to call.

I punched in the number she'd left and waited, still trying to reconcile the rational description of history I'd gotten a few days ago from Clyde Fontenot with the eccentricity I'd just encountered. Meg's voice jerked me out of my thoughts.

"What can I do for you?" I asked.

"I'm sorry to bother you, but David said there was a copy of Swanton's *Indians of the Southeast* I could borrow but we couldn't find it here and he said maybe you'd taken it home. The library's copy is checked out and . . ."

"I took it home a couple of days ago," I said. "I can bring it in Monday, or you can come by and pick it up."

"Would it be a lot of trouble if I came by your house?"

I sensed the enthusiasm in her voice and smiled to myself.

"Why don't you come by in an hour?" I said and gave her the address.

I finished up a few things at the office, picked up a hamburger at Burger King, and then drove home. It was two o'clock, and the few fishermen along the cypress lake were hunched down under their straw hats. One or two hardy souls jogged along the bike path, sweat streaming down their bodies, and when I got to the Interstate overpass, some cooler heads were parked underneath, waxing their cars. I passed the golf course, where little knots of players huddled at the holes and bounced along in their electric carts. There was a canebrake where the old railroad trestle went over the road. When I was little, I'd cut bamboo for fishing poles there. But that had been a different world.

I entered the shadow of the boulevard, with its live oaks along the median, and dodged a couple of kids on bikes. They called this the Garden District now, but it had been forty years since the elite had fled to the suburbs. A few years back the old homes had been renovated by younger couples with big dreams. But now they were turning middle-aged, and a stream of fairly constant burglaries dimmed what liberal notions they had once harbored and focused their attention on holding the line against the denizens of the ghettos to the north and west.

I parked in front of the old two-story, went in, and ran the dust rag over the mantel and the sofa arm. Digger barked for his walk, and after I obliged him, I came back, refilled his water bowl, and turned on the television. The Giants were playing the Pirates, and I got a TV tray from the kitchen and washed the hamburger down with a malt while I watched.

The chimes of the doorbell interrupted, and I gathered the malt container and wrappings, took them back to the kitchen, folded the tray, and went to the door.

The girl on the doorstep was even smaller than I remembered, with a bright, round, pixie face surrounded by black hair in a pageboy cut.

"Hi. I hope I'm not being a pain."

"Of course not. Come in." I held the door open.

"Jeez," she said, fingering the door. "Leaded glass. This reminds me of a church. Was this here when you rented it?"

"I own it," I said. "In fact, I grew up here. This house is pretty much the way my parents left it."

Her eyes widened as we passed through the living room, with its antique furniture, Queen Anne desk, and big oval mirror.

"Nice," she said. "You mean you lived here all your life?"

"My first eighteen years or so. I was away at different colleges after that, but I came back a few years ago and inherited the place."

"You live here by yourself?"

"Yes."

She frowned. "Isn't that lonely?"

I turned to look at her. From some people the questions might have been offensive, but there was an ingenuousness about her that kept me from being angry.

"Everybody gets lonely."

"I guess. No brothers and sisters?"

"No."

She stared at one of the paintings. It was of a shady country lane and it had been in the house as long as I could remember.

"I like that."

"I'm used to it, too." I turned down the television, which was the only piece of modern furniture in the room. "Can I offer you something? A Coke? A beer?"

She shook her head.

"No, thanks."

I went down the hallway to the study, where I had my desk and computer. I sensed her behind me, and when I turned to go into the room, she was still there. I went in and took the book from my desk.

"I think this is what you wanted."

She was looking around her at the bookcases made of boards and bricks and wooden crates, and the stack of books on the floor.

"What's wrong?" I asked.

"It's just this room." She shrugged as I handed her the book. "It's like an island in the rest of the house, as if this room is *you*, the way *you* are, and the rest of the house is a museum of the way things used to be."

I crossed my arms. "I guess that's pretty much so."

She gave another look around and then another little headshake.

"I talk too much. I know I make a lot of people nervous, because I say whatever pops into my head. I'm sorry."

I walked her back to the front.

"It's all right."

"Can I ask a favor? If you say no I won't be mad."

"What is it?" I asked, not sure whether to be alarmed or amused.

"I'd like to learn some of the local pottery types. If I had a key to the lab, I could spend some time there at night . . ."

I considered for a moment and then went back into my study and got a spare office key out of the drawer.

"The alarm combination is 5532. Punch it in within thirty seconds and hit the Off button. When you leave, do the same thing but hit On. Make sure you lock yourself in."

"Thanks, Alan."

"No problem," I said, and watched her go. I'd thought it was just her energy that made people wary. Now I understood better. She was like a strange little woodsprite with a view of a person's soul. I closed the door and turned back to the room.

The next day I had dinner with Sam MacGregor and his wife, Libby, in their home on the River Road, south of town. Sam had retired from the university in the early eighties, and now he and Libby enjoyed a comfortable existence, traveling and puttering about with the grandkids on both sides. Sam was still working on his manuscript about the Tchefuncte culture, but I had the feeling he would never complete it lest it leave him without a purpose.

Sam had taught me my first archaeology course when I was an undergraduate at the state university. He was father figure to a generation of archaeologists in the Southeast and evidently enjoyed the role, with his mane of white hair and Colonel Sanders goatee. After dinner we sat on the veranda, and I told him about the project in the Felicianas and then about the strange ideas of Clyde Fontenot.

Sam laughed and reached for his bourbon and water. "Clyde hasn't changed any."

"You know him?"

"Sure. He even took a few courses while I was still teaching. Bright fellow, but he went off on tangents. Once he was into science, and then it was true crime, and then I can't remember what. Finally he had some kind of breakdown and spent some time in the asylum. Isn't the first man his students drove crazy.''

''You didn't know the Devlin family, did you?''

He shook his head. ''Never met any of 'em. I do know Senator Buell McNair, though. Biggest crook in the state. If he's in on this thing, it isn't to drown ghosts, it's to make money.''

The next morning I slept later than usual. I'd dreamed about my parents, crazy dreams in which we'd been on the way to Biloxi in the old '59 Chevy with the fins. My father was driving, his face set like he was performing an audit for one of his clients, and my mother was in the back seat with me, talking. But I wasn't sure if she was talking to him or to me or both of us, and that was when I knew there was somebody else in the car. I realized then we weren't in Biloxi, that instead we were on a freeway into a big city, one I didn't recognize, and cars were whipping past us on all sides, and I wondered who the other passenger was. He was seated next to my father, a slight man with slicked-back dark hair, and when I asked my father where we were headed, my mother just laughed and said, ''Dallas.''

And I knew who the man next to my father was and cringed.

I screamed, but no sound came as the car hurtled on toward destiny, and the louder I yelled the less sound came out until at last I woke up in the darkness staring at the ceiling.

When I got into work, everyone else was there, and David came into my office with something in his hand.

''I went by the mailbox,'' he said, laying it before me. ''Bombast must've walked it through. It's our notice to proceed.''

# ▒ NINE

We started the project two days later. We went up in two vehicles and set up our base on the McNair property near where my tires had been cut. The field crew would operate in teams of three. David and Frank Hill each took two crew members and started by crossing over to the Devlin property on the west side of the creek, hoping to get that half done before any questions could be raised. Then I took one of the vehicles, the red Blazer, and drove to the courthouse in Clinton with Esmerelda so she could begin the title work. I checked at the sheriff's office about my tires and was told there was nothing to report. I asked if the sheriff was in and was told he was.

When he came out to the counter, I was surprised. He was a youngish man in a business suit, a far cry from the cowboy type I expected. I introduced myself and he nodded.

"Pat Staples," he said, shaking my hand. "I hear you had a little trouble over on the McNair property the other day." He smiled, blue eyes never wavering from my face, and I nodded.

"I have my crew out there now," I said. "I just wanted to let you know. It seems like that tract has some bad history." The sheriff picked up a paperweight of the Lincoln Memorial and balanced it on his hand. I noticed he had thin, delicate fingers, more like a pianist than a lawman.

"You mean the Doug Devlin business."

"That's right."

"These things happen. You expecting something like that to happen again?"

"You tell me."

He shrugged. "I'll send a deputy to check on your people every couple of hours, how's that?"

"I'd appreciate it."

"Now, when you're across the creek, on the Devlin land, you'll have to talk to Sheriff Cooney in St. Francisville. That's his parish."

"I hear that was a problem with the original investigation."

"Things like that never help. Cooney's a fixture, been in there forever, has his own way of handling things. I came from the DEA and I have another way. But I don't know it would've made any difference."

"You think it was a poacher?"

He sighed. "It's as good a theory as any. You've got to understand, Mr. Graham, if a killing isn't solved inside of forty-eight hours, it gets cold pretty quick. Investigations generally aren't Sherlock Holmes and fingerprints. You talk to everybody that knew the victim to see who had a motive. Then you sit by the phone and wait for somebody that doesn't like the perpetrator to call you. If that doesn't happen, your odds of solving it are nil." He held up the paperweight. "Now, in this case, nobody called and there wasn't any motive for anybody close to the man to do it, unless you count his brother. But his brother was stationed out of the country then. What was left?"

"I'm sure you looked into Doug Devlin's financial affairs."

"Doug Devlin wasn't a resident of this parish. He was just *killed* here. But from what I heard, he was doing okay. His farm wasn't bringing in much, but he was making it. He was a pretty good businessman, I guess."

"And his widow? Is she making it?"

"I hear it's tough. But then, it generally is for folks in these parts."

"Not for the McNair brothers."

"Some people do better than others."

"Does that worry you?" I asked.

"Everything about life worries me. There isn't anything I can do about most of it. Anything else?"

"One thing: Your deputy told me to watch out for a fellow named Blake Curtin. That your advice, too?"

The lawman shook his head.

"Blake's a funny cuss, but I've never known him to hurt anybody. What else can I say?"

Esmerelda told me she'd be busy in the courthouse most of the day, so I left her to her work and drove back to the survey area. Things seemed to be going well. The field crews were well along, and every so often I heard someone yell in the distance, though the wooded nature of the terrain made it impossible to see anyone. I checked the sky: There were some white, fleecy clouds, and I wondered if we might get a storm in the afternoon. If so, we'd have to pull out until the lightning was over. I knew it would complicate matters for me to grab a shovel and hand screen and try to catch up with the crew. Maybe there was something else I could take care of.

Going to St. Francisville to talk to Sheriff Cooney was out: I'd dealt with him two years earlier in connection with some Tunica burials and a murder, and he'd told me not to interfere again.

Then I remembered my dream and the sinister figure of Lee Oswald in the front seat of the car. I knew then what I was going to do.

Maybe I could claim I was helping Esmerelda.

The mental hospital was set back from the road along a tree-shaded drive. I told the guard at the gate I was there to see Dr. Childe. He took my plate number and told me to go to the three-story white building with the dome.

I parked at the side of the structure and went up the marble steps and inside to the reception office. There I handed a dour-faced woman at the desk my card and asked if Dr. Childe was available.

She asked if I had an appointment, and when I said I didn't, she frowned to let me know I was presuming on her good nature.

"I'm sorry," I said meekly, and she gave a little headshake, as if to let me know that they all said that. She lifted the phone and told someone that a Mr. Graham was here without an appointment and wanted to see the doctor. She emphasized the *mister*, as if to let me know the Ph.D. on my card didn't fool her a bit.

She directed me down the hallway to an office on the right, where I found a blond young woman whose smile compensated for that of the first receptionist.

"Would you like to wait?" she asked. "He's at a staff meeting, but he ought to be out in a few minutes."

I thanked her and picked up a copy of the latest *Archives of Psychiatry*. A few minutes into an article on bi-polar affective disorder I heard footsteps in the hall outside. A man in a white lab coat came in and handed the secretary a folder.

"Dr. Childe, this gentleman is waiting to see you," she said.

The psychiatrist turned slowly in my direction, and I saw a big man with a brown, curly beard and a belly that crept over his belt.

"Alvin Childe." The doctor held out a big hand. "How can I help you?"

I rose, noticing as I did that I still had to look up at him.

"Is there someplace we could talk?"

"Surely." He led me past the desk to a door at the rear.

"Oh," he said, turning back to the woman. "Call Gene McNair and tell him I'll be a few minutes late for lunch."

We entered an office that contained a big oak desk and some bookshelves. A couple of chairs looked like refugees from state surplus, and there was, to my surprise, no couch.

"You're the archaeologist," the physician began, settling behind his desk. I noticed a stack of files in the plastic in-basket and a legal pad open in front of him.

"Yes, sir."

"Gene McNair told me. We hunt together. He told me you were doing the historical research on the Devlin and McNair tracts. Find anything interesting?"

"Just a ghost," I said.

"Well, that ought to make the newspapers." He took off

his bifocals and leaned back. I judged his age at fifty, but he could have been five years either way.

"Lee Oswald," I said. "Everybody in town seems to think he haunts that land."

The psychiatrist nodded. "I've heard the story. But you didn't come to me about that. I'm not a parapsychologist."

"No, but you're an expert on human behavior. Why would people keep a story like that current?"

"People have psychic needs. They need to be able to make sense of the incomprehensible. Not only the philosophical unknown, like the afterlife, but things that happen in our own world, like the killing of a president. How could one little man with a rifle have so much of an influence on our world? So they invent their own explanations."

"You think Oswald acted alone."

"That's my impression. You see, with all the talk about him coming here, I did a little reading not long after I took over as director. That was four years ago. Everybody was saying he came here to apply for a job, for instance, and I wondered if maybe he had. If so, if Lee Harvey Oswald had submitted an application here and been turned down, it was one of those ironic things. Because if he'd been accepted, then maybe he'd have been working here instead of in Dallas when President Kennedy went there that day."

"And was there an application on file?"

"No. The records from that long ago had been thrown out. But he may have applied. And it might have been a good place for him. If he'd worked here, maybe one of the staff would have realized how disturbed he was and gotten him some help."

"Do you think he was psychotic?"

"He certainly had delusions of grandeur and a persecution complex. But it was more like a character disorder than what we'd label a psychosis. He was a very isolated, alienated individual. He had an overbearing mother and no father. His whole short life was dedicated to showing people he was really somebody." The doctor shook his head. "I don't know if it matters what label we use, but he was unstable, that much is sure."

"And you think he could have been helped here?"

"It's possible. Depending on *him*, of course. To be helped a person has to realize there's a problem to begin with. From what I remember, his behavior was getting more and more disorganized that year. He lost jobs, was having periods of depression, his wife was pregnant a second time, he was even trying to get back to Russia again because nothing was working for him over here. It's possible, if he'd have met the right therapist, something could have been done. It would have been worth a try."

"Maybe that's why he came to the hospital to begin with," I said. "Maybe getting the job was just an excuse."

"I've thought about that. People often use a pretense to look for help."

"I suppose."

"I've told myself it would have been an interesting case to have treated," said the big man. "Except that most of the interest in him derives from what he ended up doing. If he'd been caught before that happened, he'd have been just like any of a few million other cases."

"You mean the existential *angst*."

"Sure. It's easy to feel isolated, adrift in the world we live in, especially if you don't have close relations or the ones you do have are estranged."

I shifted in my chair. "Most of us feel alone sometimes. But we don't take a gun and shoot somebody."

"No. But which one of us knows what we're capable of? Until after we do it, I mean."

"I guess you have a point."

Dr. Childe put his hands behind his head and leaned back in his chair. "I was in anatomy lab when I heard."

"Pardon?"

"About the president being shot: I was in anatomy lab. I was in premed. The bell rang, and I went out into the hall. It was two o'clock. Somebody came up to me in the hall and said, 'The president's been killed.' I didn't believe it at first. Then somebody else came up and said, 'They got Johnson, too.' For a little while it looked like they'd killed everybody. Of course, only the first story turned out to be true."

He exhaled slowly and then reached into his desk drawer

and came up with a cigar. He held it toward me, but I shook my head, so he lit up.

"You know, I don't remember much more about that year," he said.

I looked out of the window and imagined I saw boys at play, rolling in the dirt.

"Mr. Graham?"

I looked back at the doctor. "Yes?"

"Is everything all right?"

"Yes. I was just remembering something. Funny, I hadn't thought about it for years."

"Yes, these epochal events tend to blot out the more trivial memories sometimes. Or sometimes they reach out and protect us from them. From the look on your face, it must have been something you considered important at the time."

I managed a smile.

"Just a fight I had with another boy that year. His name was Ernie Slagle." I shook my head. "I hadn't thought about him for years."

"What were you fighting about?"

"That's the funny thing: I can't even remember. I just remember I wanted to kill him at the time. I can't remember ever having felt that way about anybody."

"Well, children have strong emotions. When we get older, most of us learn how to handle them."

"Yes."

I got up.

"Thanks for your time, Doctor. I just had an itch and I needed to scratch it."

"No problem. Let me know if you find anything on that stretch you're surveying. I've hunted that land a good bit and I never saw anything archaeological, but then I'm just a headshrinker, not an archaeologist."

He followed me to the door, where I turned.

"By the way, Dr. Childe, do you know a man named Clyde Fontenot?"

Childe nodded gravely. "Yes."

"How would you characterize his ideas?"

The doctor took his cigar out of his mouth and exhaled

blue smoke. "*Different.* Nice meeting you, Mr. Graham."

I walked down the cool hallway and out of the old building, feeling the shadows of all who had ever been interned there reach out and clutch at me. When I reached my Blazer, I sat there breathing heavily for a few seconds and then started the motor.

Halfway to the survey area the image of that childhood fight sprang back into my consciousness, and I jerked the wheel to keep from leaving the road.

In my memory I was on the playground with him, pounding his face with my fists, and he was laughing at me with that sardonic, supercilious sneer.

But it wasn't the face of Ernie Slagle, it was the face of someone else, someone I had never met.

It was the face of the assassin, Lee Oswald.

# ☰ TEN

It was noon when I got back to the project area. I crossed the creek to the Devlin property and found both crews seated in the shade of an oak tree, having lunch. The day had stayed cloudy, and I was glad to see that no one looked like a case of heat exhaustion.

"Anything interesting?" I asked.

David reached into his shirt pocket and held out a plastic Ziploc bag.

"One chert flake so far. Indians didn't like this place. Must've been too far from the road."

I smiled. "Nothing else?"

"Lots of beer cans. Looks like plenty of hunters have used this land. There's a deer stand about a half-mile north of here, but there're piles of trash all over the place. Of course, some of it may have floated up during high water, but most of it's too high up for that. And it looks like the locals heard about us, because somebody's been pothunting. I found a bunch of fresh holes we didn't make."

I shook my head. It was the old story: Once people heard you were searching an area, their imagination ran to gold and silver and pirate treasure.

"Dr. Graham . . ." It was Meg speaking now, her voice so low I wasn't sure she'd said my name. "Will everybody laugh if I say something?"

"Probably," Frank said, and a couple of the others smiled,

"What is it, Meg?" I asked, squatting on the ground.

"Well, I was down by the creek, at the end of my transect, and I kept getting a funny feeling."

"Oh, oh," Frank said. "Was it like things crawling up your legs?"

"Let her talk," David shushed. "What do you mean?"

She gave him a nod of gratitude. "I can't explain it. It was like somebody, or some*thing*, was watching me from up on the other side of the hill, across the creek. When I turned around to go back uphill, I felt like there were eyes on my back. A couple of times I turned around and I thought I saw the bushes move . . ."

"Wild pigs," Frank said. "You're just about a mouthful for them."

"Shut up," David said. "But he's right. It could've been hogs. Or deer."

"I don't know. Somehow it felt . . . well, I can't describe it."

Frank rolled his eyes and started humming the theme from the *Twilight Zone*. The others chuckled.

David said, "I'll take your transect after lunch. You switch with me."

"That isn't necessary," she protested.

"It's okay."

I got up slowly, remembering that I hadn't eaten yet. My sandwich was in the cooler in the Blazer, and I started back for it. As I did, I saw a blur of movement through the windshield of the vehicle, someone who'd been behind it, on the trail. I started forward at a trot.

"Hey!"

I heard noise ahead and feet pounding along the path. I stopped and ran back to the Blazer. Maybe I should've got one of the others, but there wasn't time. I got into the vehicle, started the engine, and turned around. But the track was narrow, and it took me thirty seconds, and by that time I heard the noise of another motor starting down the trail toward the road. I urged the Blazer forward over the ruts in time to see a thin pall of dust floating toward me over the tracks.

It was another couple of minutes before I reached the highway, and when I did, I saw the vehicle in the distance, headed south. I couldn't make out the license, but I could see the color, red, and the fact that it was a truck with a camper.

Blake Curtin.

There was no sense in killing myself on the highway, so I held myself to a sedate fifty and drove back to Jackson, where I stopped at the post office. A frowning Adolph Dewey watched me enter.

"You look all het up. What you people do, hit a gold mine out there?"

"Can you tell me how to get to Blake Curtin's place?"

"Curtin?" He scratched his jaw. "Sure. But you may not want to. Man ain't all there. Might be dangerous."

"The sheriff said he was harmless."

Dewey snorted. "Yeah, well, what does he know? He was one of them drug agents before he got elected here." He leaned toward me over the counter. "Matter of fact, he got elected because he broke up a drug ring. Old sheriff resigned and Staples come in a special election a year and a half ago."

"I seem to remember hearing something about that."

"Had a big shootout, killed the main man, so I guess nobody'll ever know all that was going on. They figured a lot of folks was involved, though, because they had a warrant and they was checking all the mail for a while going to this particular party." He sighed. "That's the trouble with Staples. Does everything like in the city. Out here people don't go for all that legal crap. Old sheriff would've got to the bottom of it without warrants."

"Well, if I was crazy enough to want to find Curtin, where would I go?"

"It's your neck. He's on Highway 68 about a mile south of the intersection. Trailer on the right."

I thanked him and drove to the intersection, then went south along the narrow two-lane. I still wasn't sure what I was going to say to Blake Curtin. But so far he hadn't been willing to face me, and I had a feeling the sheriff was right about his not being dangerous.

The trailer sat on a little knoll in the middle of a chicken yard. The pickup was outside, but there was no sign of the driver. I turned in and got out of the Blazer, watching for dogs. A couple of hens pecked the dirt and some ducks waddled around in the backyard. The trailer had seen better days, and one window was taped where the glass had cracked. Trash of various kinds had been tossed underneath, and as I neared the steps, a brindled cat slouched away into the shadows. I figured the area under the trailer was a good place for mice.

I went up to the door and knocked.

"Mr. Curtin."

No answer, but I heard the reedy sound of a radio somewhere inside playing country music.

I knocked and called out again. Again no answer.

Maybe, I thought, he hadn't heard, so I pulled the door and it opened outward.

A smell of rotting food assailed me and I flinched. Mixed with it was the odor of dirty clothes and tobacco smoke.

"Mr. Curtin, are you in there?"

Sudden dread enveloped me and my head swam. Suppose he was inside, hurt or dying? I didn't know the man, had no reason to intrude upon his living quarters. But I remembered the story of Doug Devlin lying beside the stream, and how Curtin had run away from me twice, as if he knew something dangerous.

I stepped inside the dark trailer, trying to breathe through my nose.

"Mr. Curtin, my name is Alan Graham. May I come in?"

No answer, only the radio.

As my eyes adjusted, I looked around.

Pots and pans crowded the sink and roaches scurried away. A pair of blue jeans lay in the middle of the corridor leading to the sleeping compartment at the rear. The radio seemed to be coming from there.

I started down the narrow hallway, my hand outstretched.

"Mr. Curtin?"

I came to the sleeping cubicle, but it was empty. The bed was unmade. The radio was an old Channelmaster with shortwave and FM capability. It sat on a shelf along with a couple of magazines and a half-empty bottle of Evan Williams.

That was when my eyes hit on the small framed photograph beside the bed.

An old man with a white mustache posed holding up the head of a five-pronged buck, while another, younger man stood on the other side. The old man wore a checkered shirt and padded vest, but the younger one had on a fatigue cap of the kind marines wear and an olive field jacket and I could barely make out his name on the front: CURTIN. I picked up the photograph and slid it out of the frame. There was an inscription on the back: *Timothy and Blake, 1/15/62.*

Timothy Devlin, the father of Doug and Buck.

But Doug wasn't in the photo, which meant he had probably taken it.

I slipped the picture back into the frame and stuck the frame back onto the shelf. I started back down the hallway, aware now that there was no dead man here, no one in need of my help, and I was intruding.

I was almost to the door when I heard the noise outside and froze.

The door opened, and suddenly I was looking into the eyes of Blake Curtin. His hair had gone gray and his skin had tightened over his face, but there was no mistaking the features. For an instant his mouth hung half open, and then he slammed the door and I heard him running. I opened the door in time to see him turning his truck around in the front yard, and by the time I got to my own vehicle he was gone.

I returned to the survey area, crossed the creek, and was halfway up the hill when I heard yells in the woods and wondered what was going on. Then the bushes parted in front of me and David stepped out, his eyes excited.

"Alan, you're just in time. We found a site. Probably Archaic, from the scrapers and points. I was just coming back to get some more plastic bags. Looks like it may be pretty undisturbed."

The news drove thoughts of Blake Curtin out of my mind.

"That's good." It was always exciting to find a site, and an Archaic site, dating four to eight thousand years ago, was especially interesting. Nor could the business side be ignored: There was always the chance of getting a modification of the delivery order, allowing us to add money for excavation.

I followed him downslope, across the creek, and up the hillside, then through the bushes and along a game trail. The clouds had burned away somewhat with the afternoon, but there was still a chance of rain, and I wanted to make sure we didn't get involved in something we'd have to shut down because of lightning.

The site was on a little knoll, where a feeder stream trickled down toward the creek. The crew was sitting around in the shade, waiting for David, and they stood as I approached.

"Actually, Meg found it," David explained. "I can't understand, either. I put in a test hole not ten feet away. Then she hit some flakes, and when we started to make our testing grid I hit a deposit not two feet from where I'd just dug."

"Luck," Meg smiled.

"Woman's luck," Frank said sourly.

"Well, whoever's luck, it's a good find." I examined a projectile point. It was a kind called Gary, which popped up through much of the prehistoric period, but as I looked over the scraping tools and tiny stone awls, I realized David was probably right about their age.

For the rest of the afternoon we whacked bush with machetes so we could see what we were doing and then worked to define the site, which meant digging holes at specified intervals until we stopped finding artifacts. David set out taking photographs from several angles, and when he'd finished Frank asked me when we were going to put in test units.

"Later," I told him. "The site'll keep. The important thing just now is to define its boundaries and then finish the survey. Otherwise we could get bogged down in something that turns into a major project and find ourselves behind on what they sent us here to do." And, I didn't need to add, lose money in the process.

His face fell and so did the faces of some of the others, but Meg seemed cheerful enough.

"Where should we pick up our survey?" she asked.

I glanced over the maps and then checked my watch. It was two-thirty, which meant another couple of hours, if the weather held. I pointed to the northeast sector of the Devlin tract.

"Let's see if we can finish that part today," I said. Meg rose, and I saw a couple of the guys exchange alarmed looks. It was clear she could go forever. Even though it was near the end of the day, I didn't want to wear them out. There would be a need for them tomorrow. Besides, a crew member who outshone the others could cause trouble.

"Meg, you stay here," I said. "You can help David and me finish up the site map."

She shrugged. "Whatever, boss." The others melted away down the trail, and I smiled to myself. There was no mistaking their secret relief. David took out his clipboard and tossed me the measuring tape.

"Here." I let Meg have one end and watched her pace to the end of the shovel holes. I looked down at the number on the tape and called out a reading, which David transferred to the map. By three o'clock we'd gotten enough for a sketch map. We loaded our packs with the plastic artifact bags and took them back across the creek and up the other side of the valley to the vehicles and carefully placed the bags in a crate in David's Land Rover.

Then I remembered we'd left our shovels.

"I'll go get the tools," I said.

David and Meg started forward, but I shook my head.

"Let Meg come with me. I'd rather somebody stayed here with the vehicles, especially since we've got artifacts in them." I thought of Blake Curtin. I wasn't at all sure he had anything to do with cutting my tires, but he'd certainly been acting suspiciously.

David shrugged. "Sure. I've got some field notes to finish." As Meg and I started back down the track, I heard the distant rumble of thunder. I looked up. The fluffy clouds had given way to darker bolls. We were going to have a summer squall before much longer.

We splashed across the creek and started up the hill, and I heard more thunder, nearer this time.

"I think we're going to get wet," Meg quipped.

I nodded and puffed to keep up with her.

"The rain won't melt me," I said, "but I don't like lightning."

We reached the site and set about to gather up the shovels. There were only a couple of them, hers and David's, but there was also a soil probe and a bush ax and the two hand screens, which were wood frames with window mesh tacked to the bottom, used for sifting dirt.

"I think this is it," I said, giving a last look around. An explosion of thunder shook the valley then, accompanied by a flash.

I dropped a shovel and swore as I reached to pick it up. At the same time, a patter of raindrops pelted down. We stumbled along the trail, the rain blowing against us. The lightning came at quicker intervals now, the flash and the sound simultaneous. I thought of the others and hoped they had found a safe place to crouch, away from the hill crest.

The trail had turned slick as the rain mixed with the clay, and I watched Meg do a balancing act. Several times she dropped tools, but each time she managed to pick them up and keep going. I fell down once behind her and was glad the noise of the storm kept her from hearing. We lurched into the forest, where the rain sifted down in a fine spray. A branch crashed to the ground ahead of us, and Meg jumped.

Ahead was a clearing, and we came out into it and stopped. The cabin loomed ahead of us, lonely in the storm.

There was no time to worry about ghost stories.

I pointed to it and we raced for its shelter.

# ☰ ELEVEN

When we reached the cabin, my pants were smeared with red clay, and water had seeped into my boots.

"Quick," she said, "inside."

She hopped onto the sagging porch, and I followed just as lightning split a tree downhill from us. I swore and dropped my shovel and screen next to hers on the boards. Water rained down off her straw hat and she smiled.

"Home, sweet home."

I tried to grin and failed. The inside was dark and smelled of dust. Water dripped from a dozen places, but we found a corner that was dry and sat together with our backs against the wall. Overhead, the rain beat a tattoo on the corrugated roof.

"I wonder who used to live here?" she asked.

So I told her.

"The kids have it all figured out. Oswald's ghost stays here. Hell, he may even be in here with us right now."

I was thinking of her comment earlier that someone had been watching. But she surprised me.

"No, I don't think so," she said.

I laughed. "Well, it's just a story."

"I know. But I'm psychic and I don't feel a thing."

"You're psychic?"

"That's what some of my friends say." She stretched her arms out in front of her. "They say I know things nobody else does. That I have intuition. I think that part's right, but I don't really think I'm psychic. I think I just tend to see some things other people miss. Anyway, I don't see anything here but an old shack.''

"That's good. Because if there is a ghost in here, there's no place for us to go until the rain quits.''

She pulled a stick of beef jerky out of her shirt pocket and offered me some. I took a pinch, and she nibbled on the rest.

"How did you get into contract archaeology?'' she asked. "If I'm not being nosy.''

I told her about Sam MacGregor and how he'd been a substitute father. "Of course, my father didn't die until a few years ago, but I was still closer to Sam in a lot of ways.''

"You haven't ever held a teaching job?''

"Once, out west. But I was strung out with personal problems at the time. And besides, they said my teaching was too unorthodox. I didn't get tenure.''

"Too unorthodox,'' she reflected. "Dangerous words.''

"Yeah. Well, not too many of the senior faculty would come to class dressed in a gorilla suit to teach hominid evolution.''

She giggled. "I love it. I can just see old Godfrey in the department here if that happened.'' She cocked her head. "So why did you first study archaeology? Was that due to Sam MacGregor, too?''

I shook my head. "He provided a means, but I'd pretty well decided while I was in high school what I wanted to be.''

"The romance of it,'' she said.

I tried to think back to that time in my life.

"Actually, I think I just decided the past was a better time to be in than the present.''

"Heavy.'' A stray raindrop flew in through one of the broken windows and stung my face. "You keep your house like a museum, except for your own little island in it, and you like the past better than the present. Ever talked to a shrink, Alan?'' She giggled, but I cut her off.

"Just a couple of hours ago, as a matter of fact.''

"Are you serious?''

"Perfectly.''

She assessed me with her big brown eyes, and then we started laughing together.

"It sounds like the rain's about quit," I said then and forced myself up. I went over to the door in time to see a bedraggled Frank Hill straggle into the clearing, his clothes soaked.

"Jeez," Frank said. "A nice cozy place to stay and here we were in a damned hurricane." He gave Meg a mistrusting glance. "Some people have all the luck."

I smiled, clapped him on the shoulder, and we started back across the valley toward the vehicles. Once on the highway, he and the others pulled into a store to pick up Cokes, but I waved and kept going, eager to get home.

Three hours later, after a hot bath and a toddy, I sat in the living room, leafing through the television guide. No good old film noirs, I noticed, and I threw the booklet down in disgust.

I looked around me. So I kept the place neat and only used the living room to watch TV and to entertain my very infrequent guests. Did that make it a damned museum? The furniture had all been left to me by my parents. There was a Queen Anne desk and a Chippendale chair and some Wedgwood china in a cabinet against one wall. There was a rosewood table, its wings folded so that it fitted just under the window. The brick fireplace harbored an ancient gas contraption of iron with fake briquettes that radiated heat.

These were the artifacts of my childhood, the surroundings that lent me comfort. Other people held estate sales or passed furniture on to covetous relatives. I kept mine *in situ*, like the archaeologist I was.

Pepper had mentioned it, but I'd shrugged it off. After all, being neat wasn't against the law.

I got up slowly and went up the stairs to the second story.

The old boards creaked as they took my weight, and I imagined I could hear my mother's voice calling out to ask who it was. It was real, and yet the last time I had heard it was twenty years ago.

Their bedroom was the first door to the left, across the hall from my own. I seldom went in there, because there was nothing in it I needed. I opened the door slowly now, not sure what I expected to find on the other side.

But it was just the way it had always been: The big four-poster bed with the chintz spread, the mahogany dresser in one corner, the armoire in the other, a small *prie-dieu* beside the closet door.

My mother had become more devout in her last years and had spent hours on her knees on the *prie-dieu*, and when I opened the closet door, I saw a church calendar from 1972 with a print of Jesus and his bleeding heart.

Then I looked at the clothes.

His were still there: two summer suits, one linen and one seersucker, and several of synthetic material for the rest of the year. There was also an old Army uniform, with his lieutenant's bars still in place.

Of course, her clothes had been gone long since, because he had gotten rid of them a year or so after her death.

I didn't look in the dresser because I knew what I would find: his razors and some cologne and an assortment of silk ties. There was also the wallet he'd had with him the day he died.

My father had installed central air a couple of years before his death, and the room smelled like mothballs, despite the slow breeze that drifted in from the vent. I went to the little bedside table and lifted the photograph with the gold frame. It showed them on their wedding day in 1946, right after the war. They seemed very happy.

I put the photo down and reminded myself to mention to the once-a-week cleaning lady that the room needed dusting. Then I went back down, settled in my chair, and tried the TV again. Halfway through some movie I fell asleep, and when I awoke the phone was ringing.

I looked around, surprised. It was dark already, and the clock on the mantel said ten-thirty. I found the phone and picked it up.

"Yes?"

"Alan . . ." It was Meg's voice at the other end. "Alan, you've got to come here in a hurry. I'm at the lab . . . I . . ." Her voice caught, and then the line went dead.

It took me six minutes to make the drive from my house to the office. When I got there, I saw flashing red lights outside, and my stomach did a flip. I pulled in behind a police cruiser and was halfway up the walk when an arm reached out to stop me.

"Who are you?"

"My name is Graham. This is my office." That was when I saw the ambulance. The paramedics were trotting across the lawn with their bags.

"You can't go in there, sir," the policeman was saying, but I pushed past him into the lab.

Trays of artifacts had been scattered on the floor and chairs had been overturned. But what got my attention was the paramedics, who were bending over something on the floor. I sagged against the door frame.

"My God," I mumbled.

The policeman was guiding me outside. I was trembling, and I wondered idly if the weather had suddenly turned cold. Two minutes later the medics came out with a stretcher, and I saw an oxygen mask fixed over Meg's face.

"How is she?" I asked, but nobody said anything.

Ten minutes later a couple of detectives came and took my statement. From what little they told me, Meg had been shot by someone who had forced open the back door. The alarm had been on, and the clerk at ADT had called the police, who had, surprisingly, arrived a couple of minutes before I did.

I went inside and viewed the mess. There was a spot of blood on the floor where she'd fallen, and I cursed myself for agreeing to let her work late.

One of the detectives picked up something from the floor.

"Recognize this?"

It was a brass cartridge casing.

"Yes. It's one of our artifacts."

"Artifact?" He gave me a funny look.

"That's right. See the dirt inside it? My crew probably picked it up on site today. Meg was getting ready to clean it along with the other things."

"What kind of work do you people do?"

I told him. "Sometimes old artifacts and more recent

ones are found together. This looks like stuff they picked up from the surface. There was an Indian site, but there was also probably a hunter out there shooting his gun sometime in the last twenty years or so.''

The detective held the brass tube up to the light.

''Round for a deer gun,'' he said. ''Probably from a war surplus rifle.''

Something in my brain went on alert.

''War surplus?''

''Right. 6.5 millimeter. Like one of those old Italian rifles.''

# ▰▰TWELVE

I spent the rest of the night at the hospital. I signed papers that committed the firm in ways that would make Marilyn blench, but by midnight, when they decided to put the patient in a private room, I knew at least that the bullet hadn't hit anything vital and that Meg would pull through.

That was when I called her folks in Maryland. It wasn't an easy call to make, and I spent most of the time apologizing and promising to take care of all expenses.

What kind of a neighborhood was our business located in, anyway? Well, there were worse . . . What good was an alarm system if people broke in? A very good point, but it hadn't ever happened before. What was she doing working by herself at night? Bad judgment on my part . . .

I went upstairs to her room and sat down in the padded chair beside the bed. They'd taken away the breathing apparatus, and she was sleeping under a heavy dose of sedatives. The bullet had hit her shoulder and glanced off in an odd direction.

My God, what was going on? I didn't believe that it was a random housebreaking. Somebody had tried to get in, either to silence her or to steal something we had. I thought it was more likely to be the latter. But what could we have discovered?

Then I remembered the cartridge cases.

But they had lain on the ground for years. There could hardly be anything important about them. They had probably been fired by Doug Devlin, who had had that caliber rifle. So it must be something else. Or was it supposed to be a warning? An escalation in a chain that had started with the cutting of my tires?

I drifted off to sleep in the chair, floating somewhere above the bed and looking down on her as she lay there, a child with a pixie face, strangely different in repose . . .

The last time I'd spent the night in a hospital had been while my father was dying. I'd made a bed downstairs on a couple of chairs in the waiting room of the intensive care unit, afraid to sleep and unable not to. It was a sad, anxious place, with little groups of family members clotted about like blood, waiting to hear. Some read, some played cards, and some stretched out to sleep.

How many nights had I spent there? Two? Three? I could never remember, because afterward all the minutes and hours and days blended together into a single gray image of exhaustion.

It was just turning to light outside when I heard Meg stirring.

"Alan?"

I looked over at her and saw her eyes on me, questioning.

"Where am I?"

I reached out and gave her hand a squeeze.

"You're okay. You had an accident but everything's okay. You're in the hospital."

"Hospital?"

She tried to move her right arm and groaned.

"What happened?"

"You were working late in the lab. You called me, said for me to come. When I got there, they said you'd been shot."

"Shot?" She frowned. "I can't remember. I just remember sitting in that old camp house with you, and the rain falling, but after that . . ."

"Don't worry, it'll come in time."

An hour later I left her sleeping and went home. My eyes felt like sand, and I moved like a man dragging an anchor. I took a warm bath and went to sleep in the tub. When I awoke the phone was ringing again, and when I reached it I heard Marilyn's indignant voice.

"Alan, do you have any idea what you did? You let me walk into this mess this morning, and I called the police. They told me what happened last night and said you'd been here. Why in the hell didn't you call me instead of letting me just stumble into it?"

I apologized for the second time today.

"I meant to be in by now to explain," I said. "I lost track of the time."

She harrumphed and hung up.

When I got in, David and a couple of the students had managed to replace the artifacts in the proper trays, although one tray had been hopelessly scrambled. I was still staring down at the disaster when the phone rang and I heard the dreaded words:

"Alan, this is Bertha Bomberg." My blood turned to ice.

"Yes, Bertha."

"How did things go yesterday?"

I thought about Meg in the hospital. "All right during the fieldwork."

"What does that mean?"

"We found a prehistoric site, probably Archaic."

"And?"

"And somebody broke into the lab last night and tried to kill one of our people."

"Well, you aren't located in the best part of town. Is everything okay now?"

"More or less. The employee is in the hospital. They say she'll be all right. We've managed to re-sort most of what was in the trays."

"Most?"

"One tray was pretty well scrambled. We'll probably never sort those things out again."

"Was that from the site?"

"Yes."

"How to you plan to deal with it?"

"I guess we'll just have to collect some more artifacts and label these as part of a general collection."

I heard an intake of breath.

"I don't like the sound of that."

"Bertha, for God's sake . . ."

"And what about today? Do you have people in the field?"

"We called it off. This doesn't happen every day."

"Alan, I'm not trying to upset you, but it's only fair to tell you that when the next contracts are bid, this may be a factor. This doesn't happen at CEI or Pyramid."

"Anything else, Bertha?"

"Nothing right now. I'm getting my schedule together for the next couple of weeks. I'll call you when I'm coming up for a site visit."

"We'll look forward to it."

I pressed the receiver back down and took some deep breaths, waiting for my blood pressure to subside.

David came in and put a friendly hand on my shoulder.

"Look, I'll try to make sense out of that last tray. You go home and get some rest. I'll call everybody and tell them to show up for the field tomorrow."

I nodded. "Good idea."

I stumbled out to the Blazer. The heat was withering, and when I got in, I barely mustered the energy to start the air-conditioning. David was right: I needed to sleep. But first I went by a florist, picked up some flowers, and then drove to the hospital, parking in the lot across Hennessey Boulevard and making the hot, draining trek across the asphalt to the building. When I walked into the room, Meg was sitting up, some of the color back in her face. I put the flowers next to the bed and she smiled.

"From the crew," I said.

"They're beautiful."

"Have the cops been back?"

She nodded. "A detective named Landry. He wanted to know what happened and then he asked me why I was working by myself at night."

"Because your boss is a jerk," I said. "I'm sorry. I never thought . . ."

"It wasn't your fault."

"So exactly what did happen?" I asked. "Have you been able to remember?"

"Well, it's still only bits and pieces, but I remember working at the lab table and hearing something at the back door. It sounded like somebody was pulling on it, trying to get it open. I went back there, but I didn't see anything from the window. So I went back to the lab and then it started again. That's when I picked up the phone on the lab table and called you. Then something hit me and I woke up here.''

"Tell me, what were you working on when it happened? The stuff we found yesterday?''

She nodded. "That's right. I'd washed the collection and put it in the trays to dry, and I was putting catalogue numbers on it all. All except the metal, like the cartridge casings, because I wasn't sure how you wanted to deal with them.''

"Was there anything in the collection—anything at all— that seemed unusual?''

"Not that I could see. Just lithics. A few recent things from the surface collection, old cartridge casings and a couple of fragments of what looks like an old coffee cup. I don't know why anybody would care about any of that.''

"But somebody does.''

"Maybe it's me.''

"What?''

She fixed me with those great brown eyes.

"What if it's not the artifacts at all, but something about *me*—something I saw, for instance.''

"But what could that be? We were together most of the time. And when we weren't, you were with the others. Why are they going for *you*, and not for David or Frank or me?''

"I don't know.''

I tried to think back, but my mind was foggy from lack of sleep. "When we left the field, your group stopped at a grocery for Gatorade and Cokes, didn't you?''

"Sure.''

"Did you talk about what you were doing in the field? Could anybody in the store have gotten the impression you'd found something valuable?''

"I don't think so. The storekeeper was busy talking to the mailman when we got there. He asked us what we were doing, and David said we were archaeologists. Somebody asked us if we were looking for Lee Oswald's buried treasure and everybody laughed. David didn't say anything about the site we found, and I remember him telling us afterward, on the way home, that you never want to give anybody the impression you found anything that would be worth their while to vandalize."

I nodded. "Well, maybe the cops will get to the bottom of this. I'll come see you later."

"Thanks, Alan. You're sweet. But you know, it really wasn't your fault."

"I'm coming anyhow," I said.

When I got home, I fed Digger and fell onto my bed in my clothes. For a blessed instant I had the sensation I was floating just over the sheets and that there were other people in the house, aunts and uncles and cousins. The sounds of my parents' voices . . . I was safe and protected and so was the world, because not only were my parents alive, but so was President Kennedy. Life was golden and things came out right . . .

I must have slept hours, because it was dark outside when I awoke. The door chimes were ringing. At first I thought it was part of my dream, but then I realized there was someone outside.

I forced myself up, found my shoes, and made my way through the hallway to the living room. I halted before the ornate door, suddenly terrified. What if something had happened to Meg? What if she'd taken a turn for the worse? Or even more terrible, what if the person who had assaulted her had snuck into her room and finished the job?

It would be easy to ignore the chimes, just pretend no one was there, sink back into my comfortable cocoon . . .

I reached for the knob, yanked the door open, and froze.

The person on my doorstep was none other than Cynthia Jane Devlin, dressed like she was going to dinner.

# ▓ THIRTEEN

"I'm sorry if I woke you up," she said.

"It's okay."

"May I come in?"

I stepped back, holding the door open for her. She entered cautiously, her eyes taking in the decor, and I wondered what she was thinking. She turned to face me.

"About the other day," she began, "I acted badly. You were right, of course: I did lie about Blake. But I had my reasons. I just didn't expect you to see through me so easily."

If she had been attractive before, she was beautiful now, her hair a deep black that set off her features. She wore a gold cross, and her blouse dipped down to reveal her cleavage. I wondered if she had dressed especially for me, and if so, why?

"How did you know where I lived?" I asked.

"I went to your office. They told me about what happened last night and said you were trying to get some sleep. I started to leave, but one of your people—the pretty, little girl who seemed to be in charge—said it was all right, you'd be waking up soon. She gave me your address."

I made a mental note to talk to Marilyn.

"Sit down," I said. "Can I offer you something to drink?"

"Diet Coke, if you have it."

I went into the kitchen and came back with two cans, a Coke for her and a Dr. Pepper for myself.

"I didn't know you were an antiques collector," she

said. "Some of these pieces must be over a hundred years old."

"Sort of like a museum, huh?"

Her face crinkled into a smile. "Why would you say that?"

"No reason."

"Anyway, I'm sorry about Blake. I hope you can understand. He's a very shy man. He's had his problems, and all he wants now is to be left alone. He's got a little money from an injury settlement from Gulf States a few years ago and he just makes it on that and by doing a little handy work. I let him work at my place because he seems to enjoy it and I feel comfortable around him. Plus he provides some protection."

"And you thought I was going to upset him?"

She held the smile. "You did go to his trailer yesterday. It upset him badly."

So that was it. Was she here to find out what I'd learned?

"I'm sorry. But he was out poking around on site again. You have to admit it's suspicious when you come up on somebody and they run."

She leaned back on the sofa. "That's just his way. You have to get to know him before he'll even communicate with you. He's roamed these woods for the past forty years. He isn't going to change now."

I thought about the photograph beside his bed.

"He was friends with your husband and your father-in-law."

"Yes. Old Timothy let him have the run of the place."

"He must have had his speech then, because he was in the Marines."

She stiffened slightly. "You've done some digging."

"I'm an archaeologist," I said, trying to pass it off as a joke.

She exhaled. "There's no sense being cagey. Yes, he was in the Marines. He served his time overseas before Vietnam."

"So something happened while he was in the Marines?"

"I don't know. I just know that when I came here as Doug's bride in 1979, Blake was living here and he had a reputation as a heavy drinker. And he couldn't talk, but

Doug told me he used to be able to. He was working for Gulf States then and he had an accident on a power pole, fell down to the bottom and hurt his back. He got a worker's comp settlement. After that, he just became more and more withdrawn. But he's always been nice to me.''

"What did your husband say about him? He must have known him all his life.''

"He said some people were born shy and Blake was one of them.''

I sipped my drink, trying to sort through my thoughts. I had to phrase my next question carefully.

"Did your husband have him around as much as he is these days?''

Her brows dipped in a frown. "Do you mean was Doug jealous? The answer is no. And I don't think Blake had anything to do with his death.''

I pictured Doug Devlin lying beside the creek, his blood oozing into the sand.

"Suppose it wasn't a poacher. Was there anybody who would've wanted your husband dead? Anybody he was crosswise with over a business deal, for instance?''

She gave a little laugh. "Doug didn't have any business sense. Our income was falling off back then. Oh, every once in a while there was some money—he'd sell some cattle or something—but toward the end things weren't good. He was worried. I kept asking if he thought we ought to sell some land, but he didn't want to.''

"Your husband wasn't trained in any profession?''

"He had three years of college and dropped out. Why study when he could inherit Timothy's money and land? And as long as Buck was in the Army, nobody would be looking over his shoulder.''

"And since he's died?''

"Life is never easy,'' she said.

"No,'' I agreed.

Cyn Devlin leaned toward me. "Alan, I hope what happened to your friend last night wasn't connected with anything you're doing on the property.''

"I do, too.'' I shrugged. "But there isn't any reason it should be, is there?''

"No, just those damned stories about the cabin. I'm not superstitious, but it bothers me. It's almost like anybody who sets foot there is risking some kind of supernatural curse."

I recalled Meg's sensation that we were being watched. "I guess Curtin told you we were on the west side?"

She nodded. "He went out there this morning and saw where your people had been digging." She reached over and touched my arm. "Look, I know I was bitchy the other day, but you could have used my pasture to get back there."

"It seemed best not to raise your hackles."

She bent the can so it made a little pop, and for the first time I realized she was nervous.

"I've taken up enough of your time. I just wanted to apologize. If there's anything I can do . . ."

She got up, setting the can on a coaster, and put her hand on the door.

"Wait," I heard myself say.

She turned her head to face me. "Yes?"

"There *is* something you could do."

"Oh?"

"Take me to Blake Curtin. Tell him I just want to ask him some questions. Will you do that?"

There was a second's hesitation. "Now?"

"Now or later."

"He may not be at his trailer."

"But he'll go back there to sleep, won't he?"

She bowed her head. "Yes."

"Take me to him, and I'll buy you the best steak in town."

She shrugged in defeat. "How can I resist a deal like that?"

We ended up at Bear Corners, a restaurant on Highway 10 in downtown Jackson, a block from the post office.

"I haven't been here since Doug died," she told me as she pulled her station wagon in at the curb. "Maybe it's time to start again. Besides, it'll give people something to talk about."

When we entered, there was the usual crowd of families, and I didn't recognize any of them. She told me this was the first time she'd eaten out with a man since her husband had died, and then looked away, as if she was embarrassed. I told her archaeologists who lived in old houses and collected furniture were particularly dangerous, and she smiled. Then the smile died away, and I saw that she was staring at something over my shoulder. I glanced behind me and saw Sheriff Staples in the doorway, accompanied by a pretty, red-haired woman who must have been his wife, and a girl of eight or nine.

I turned back around.

"Everything okay?"

"Yeah." She averted her eyes.

When we left, she made sure she gave his table a wide berth. He looked up once and our eyes met, but he gave no sign that he recognized me. When we got out to the car, she opened her door and got in before I could move around to the passenger side.

She sat behind the wheel, motionless, and I sensed that she was trembling.

"What's wrong?"

"Nothing." She started the car. "I just think we better hurry if we want to catch Blake."

It was twilight as we pulled into his yard. Curtin's pickup was there, and there was a light in the trailer window. Cyn got out and I started to follow, but she held up her hand.

"Better let me handle this. He knows me."

I waited while she went up to the door and knocked. There was no answer, and she opened it and I heard her call his name. A few seconds later she came back and got a piece of paper out of her purse.

"He must have seen us coming up. He probably ran off. He's like that. I'll leave him a note telling him to come to my house in a little while. He trusts me."

I watched her scribble out a quick message and then go place it in the trailer door where Curtin would see it when he returned.

So we were going to her house. I wondered if things had just fallen out that way or whether it was part of a plan that had begun when she'd knocked on my door. I felt uneasy, but there wasn't much I could do. She had the transportation, and I could hardly wrestle the steering wheel away from her. Suddenly an unreasonable fear came into my mind: Suppose it was all a ploy to get me away from Meg? It had been Cyn's idea to take her car, *her* idea to go to Bear Corners, twenty miles away from the city, and now *her* idea to get me to her house.

What if at this very minute someone was headed for Meg's room to silence her?

But what could Meg possibly know that was worth taking those kinds of risks for? I was being paranoid. I was in the company of a beautiful woman, one with a few hangups, to be sure, but who among us didn't have them? Why not put aside my suspicions and just enjoy the evening?

The last filaments of sunlight were streaking the western sky as we slowed for her driveway. The old house squatted back from the road like an ailing creature, its window airconditioning units poking out like so many sores. I wondered how it must be for a single woman to live out here by herself. She stopped at the side of the house and cut the ignition.

"Well, we're here," she said.

I followed her up the walk, my curiosity battling a sense of foreboding that was not likely to go away until I had a chance to use the telephone.

"Make yourself at home," she invited, opening the door and flipping on a light.

I went in after her and glanced around.

We were in a big room, with a dining table that had probably once seen formal dinners. Now it was bare, with a single candlestick holder in the middle and a stack of the day's mail on the end. I recognized from the envelopes with windows that most of the day's delivery was bills.

She waved her hand at the peeling wallpaper. "I'm going to work on this room next week. I papered the sitting room last week. I figure with Blake helping me I'll eventually catch up."

I nodded and she took a step forward, her eyes suddenly blazing.

"I won't sell it. I don't care what they offer. I won't sell this place, and you can tell them if they ask."

"Nobody's asked," I said quietly.

The fight seemed to go out of her.

"Of course not. I'm sorry."

"It's all right. Look, can I use your phone?"

"It's in the parlor," she said, pointing.

I made my way over a rug that had been new when Truman was in the White House and found the phone on the wall. The furniture was not as valuable as what was in my own house, but it was respectably old, nevertheless. Old Timothy's, no doubt.

I got the number of the hospital from Directory Assistance and then dialed the main number and asked for Meg's room. My heart did a couple of hammer strokes while I waited, and then the line clicked and I heard her voice.

"Meg, are you all right?"

"Alan, is that you? Of course I am. I was just watching a rerun of *All in the Family*. The food here's goopy, but I guess I'll live. My shoulder's starting to throb now, but the doctor said not to worry. He gave me some pills."

"Well, I meant to come visit . . ."

"Don't worry about it. David's been here and Marilyn, too, and a couple of my college friends. We're going to play Clue a little later."

"Well, hold tight, kid. I'll be in to see you tomorrow, late probably."

"You're going back to the field?"

"Yeah."

There was a silence, and then I heard her voice again, sounding small over the lines.

"Alan, be careful. I have a bad feeling about this project."

We said goodbye, and I hung up in time to hear movement behind me.

I turned and saw Cyn standing in the doorway, with a strange, almost hurt look on her face, but even as I watched, the look vanished and she nodded over her shoulder.

"Blake Curtin's here," she said.

# ▰Fourteen

I walked into the living room and stopped.

The man in front of me was an apparition.

A tangle of gray hair nested on his shoulders, and black eyes regarded me nervously from deep-set sockets. His overalls were streaked with grease, and a gray stubble covered his cheeks. As I watched, his hands clawed up and down his pant legs as if he expected some terrible outcome. But above all, the impression he gave was of suffering.

"Mr. Curtin," I said, offering my hand.

His eyes went to Cyn for approval, and then he wiped a hand on his pants and stuck it out for me to shake. As our hands touched, I felt callouses on his skin and knew he was used to hard work.

"Thank you for coming," I said. "I'm sorry if I startled you yesterday. I didn't mean to."

His head made a token dip.

"But a couple of times when I've been out on the McNair tract, I've seen you running away. You've got to admit that running away makes a fellow wonder what's going on."

He gave a little shrug.

"I wouldn't be so concerned," I said, "except that somebody's slashed my tires and bashed my head. Then last night somebody broke into my office and almost killed an employee of mine."

Curtin's eyes flew to the woman. He shook his head back

and forth vigorously, and for an instant I thought he was going to bolt.

But Cyn took his arm.

"We know it wasn't you," she said. "Nobody's saying it is. Are they?"

I took the cue. "Of course not. But whatever's going on out here, I had a feeling if I could talk to you, you might be able to give me some ideas. After all, nobody knows this area better than you do."

The scarecrow gave a fleeting smile and shifted from one foot to the other. He looked over at Cyn again and she nodded.

"It's okay, Blake." She produced a pad and pencil, and he took up the writing instrument and wrote slowly on the paper, then handed it to her. She glanced down at it, then gave it to me.

*I don't know anything*, it said. *I saw you with Mr. McNair and thought you were going to arrest me.*

"Arrest you? For what? Trespassing?"

The grizzled head bobbed an affirmative.

"Then what about the other day when you came up on the other side? You ran away then, too."

The pencil moved again on the paper.

*Curious*, he wrote.

"And today?" I asked.

*The same.*

It was my turn to shrug.

"Have you ever seen or heard anything strange on the property?" I asked. "On either side of the creek?"

His eyes darted to hers, alarmed. Then he raised his hands, palms upward, and shrugged.

"No poachers? Trespassers?"

Another hint of a smile, and he wrote:

*All the time.*

"You were friends with Doug Devlin, weren't you?"

A nod.

"Were you around here when he was killed?"

He shook his head "no" vigorously.

Then I asked him the question that was really on my mind:

"You've heard the story about Lee Harvey Oswald coming here. You ever see him?"

His mouth dropped open, showing yellow teeth, and the writing pad fell to the floor. He began to tremble and wheeled to flee, but Cyn put a hand on his arm.

"There's nothing to be afraid of, Blake. Just answer the question."

He raised his hands again, as if helpless, and I waited.

His mouth moved but no sound came out.

"Don't worry," Cyn soothed. "It's okay."

He stared down at the pad as if it were a murder weapon, and I picked it up and handed it to him. He took it hesitantly, and then, in a sudden surge of fervor, wrote something and thrust it at me.

*Yes.*

"Mind telling me when and where?"

The mouth opened again, and then he wheeled and ran out of the house. A few seconds later I heard his truck start and the sound of his tires spraying shells from the drive as he headed for the highway.

"I didn't mean to upset him again," I said.

Cyn went to the sideboard and took out a bottle of bourbon and a couple of glasses.

"This isn't the first time it's happened," she said. "Do you take ice or just water?"

"Water will be fine," I said.

I followed her into the kitchen. As I stood there, I was impressed by the vastness of the place, the immenseness of its rooms, and how small she seemed.

She handed me a glass and then raised her own in a toast.

"It's nice to have somebody to drink with," she said.

All at once I understood why she had come to my house and why we had ended up here in the country in a vast and decaying house. It wasn't a plan, at least not a sinister one. It was something else very human.

"Yes," I said. "It is."

She led me back through the parlor and the living room to what appeared to have once been a sunporch but had since been enclosed and made into a den. She put an old-fashioned LP on the turntable.

"Do you like Stravinsky?" she asked.

"Yes."

A few seconds later *The Rites of Spring* came floating out over the room.

"When I grew up, all I knew was rock and country," she said. "And I've got to admit, some of it was good. But I wanted more than that. So when I married Doug, I started taking a few courses at the university. Music, for one. Doug didn't think much of the idea. Education wasn't something he ever felt a need for. But he tolerated it." She smiled bitterly. "Tolerated. What a terrible word."

"You and your husband didn't have a lot in common?"

She raised her glass and stared into it.

"Not much. I fell in love with him because I was young and he had money and it seemed like a way out. He wanted me because I was a decoration and I wasn't a threat to him." She looked up into my eyes. "And then, one day, I became one."

All the tenseness I'd sensed earlier was back, and I saw her fingers go white against the glass.

"Still," I said in a near whisper, "you loved him."

"Did I?" She set the glass down on the table and sighed. "I guess I did. You can't live with somebody that long and not feel *something*. I kept telling myself that."

"Do you still keep telling yourself?" I asked.

"Not often. Now I see him more for what he was. A bully, a drunk, lazy and ignorant. A man who was drinking in some bar when the word came about his son being killed."

"I'm sorry."

"Thank you. I'm sorry, too, for dredging all this up. I didn't mean to. I thought I'd done a pretty good job up to now."

"I think you've done a great job."

"You're nice."

"Sometimes. But I have my moments."

She stood and came over to me then.

"No, I think you're always nice. I can see it in your face."

"Can you." It was a statement.

"So who is she?" Cyn asked, surprising me.

I told her about Pepper.

"Is she coming back?" Cyn asked.

"Sure." I tried to sound certain, but the word came out strained.

"My luck," she said, pouring herself another drink. "The good ones are all taken."

I wasn't sure what to say, just watched her toss off half the glass.

"What if she doesn't come back?" she asked suddenly. "You'd be free then, right?"

It felt like a stab in the belly, and I was still hunting for words when she set her glass down hard.

"See what a bitch I am? I'm sorry."

"It's okay," I said, watching her refill her glass.

"Cyn . . ." It was the first time I'd said her name. "What was it about Staples when you saw him tonight?"

"I told you not to ask."

"I'm sorry. But you've got to admit your reaction was pretty strong."

"Then I guess I'll have to answer." Her words were a monotone, with just a touch of hopelessness.

I waited.

She looked at her glass as if trying to decide whether to drink any more and then lowered it.

"I don't like Staples. He's too smooth. Have you ever run into anybody that's too smooth? He smiles, but there's a knife behind it. He made his name around here by killing a man in a shootout on Highway 9. The man was supposed to be the head of a big dope ring. But after Staples had shot him, it turned out the man didn't have all the drug money he was supposed to be carrying and he had less than half an ounce of cocaine. Then, when Mark was killed, Staples investigated. He said Mark had been drinking. The autopsy showed a .05 level of alcohol. So Mark had had a couple of beers. He wasn't drunk, but the story made the rounds of the whole damned parish. And when Doug was killed, there wasn't any real investigation at all, because Staples and Cooney couldn't decide whose jurisdiction it was, so they ended up deciding it wasn't anybody's. They went through the motions, that's all. A poacher hunting out of season. That was the verdict. And that's what I've had to live with.''

"I'm sorry."

"Don't be. It's past."

"Is it?"

She took another healthy swallow.

"I don't know. All I know is you're going to have to spend the night here whether you want to or not, because I've had too much to drive." She giggled. "Unless you want to drive me to your place."

"Cyn . . ."

She came up against me then, raised her face, and touched her lips briefly to mine.

"It's okay. You can sleep in the extra room upstairs. I promise not to sneak in during the night."

When she finished her drink, I let her lead me up the stairs. We went down a hallway, past closed doors, to another midway along. She opened it, and I saw that it was the master bedroom.

"The door across the hall was my son's," she said. "I don't go there much. You can sleep in his bed."

I watched her door close, then went into the room across the hall, shut the door behind me, and turned on the window unit.

With ten minutes I was asleep, but sometime in the night I awoke.

Something had shaken me out of my dreams, the sound of a door opening or steps outside in the hall. Then I heard a car engine start, faint and muffled by the sounds of the air conditioner. I got up and opened the door into the hall. Cyn's door was cracked open and when I looked in, I saw her bed was empty.

The clock on the bedside table said one.

# ≡ FIFTEEN

I pulled on my pants and tried to decide what to do next. She had the only transportation, so unless I planned to walk twenty miles or could find the keys to her jeep, I might as well make up my mind to stay here.

Then I thought about Meg. *What if?*

I made my way down the hallway to the master bedroom. I turned on the light and saw a phone on the bedside table.

This was not going to make me popular.

I dialed David's number and after six rings heard him mumble a hello.

"David, I'm sorry to wake you up—"

"Alan? What the hell—?"

"I know. Look, I've got a crazy favor to ask you. You can kill me tomorrow but please do this for me now."

"Do what? Jesus, man, it's one in the frigging A.M."

"I know. But I'm stuck in the country. I've got no car."

"What?"

"Don't even ask. But I'm worried about Meg. I need you to go stay with her for a couple of hours."

"Where are you?"

"I'll tell you tomorrow. *Please.*"

He groaned. "All right. But what the hell are you expecting?"

"I don't know. Just don't let anybody that isn't a doctor or a nurse into the room."

"Like I'm a damn rent-a-cop."

"Thanks, David."

"We may be late getting on site tomorrow. Some of the crew may sleep through their alarms."

"I understand."

I hung up and sat down on the bed.

Did I really think Cyn could be using me to get to Meg? It didn't seem likely, but then, how many women left their bed at one in the morning to go driving by themselves? I rubbed my eyes and looked around the room.

It was tastefully furnished, with a mirror on the closet door and a separate chest of drawers on each side of the big bed. A gas space heater against one wall made me wonder if the big house didn't get cold in the winter. There was a dresser beside the window, and I went over to look down at it, seeking some clue to the strange personality of the woman I knew as Cyn Devlin. A quick search of the drawers showed nothing but the usual accoutrements of a woman's toilet. I turned to the chest of drawers on the left side of the bed and found her things carefully folded inside, one drawer for undergarments, one for blouses, one for shirts and pants. Nothing there.

Then I turned to the other chest, and the first thing I saw was the picture.

It was a small closeup photo framed in gold. The man in it was handsome in a beefy sort of way, the kind who had reached his peak in high school and looked like he would go to fat quickly afterward. His smile was half leer, half smirk. I decided instinctively it wasn't the face of a man I would trust.

Doug Devlin. It had to be.

I set it back down and opened the top drawer. It was empty. So were the other drawers. She had taken out all his clothing.

Nor was there anything in the closet, for when I opened the door, all I saw was her own clothing beside a clutch of empty hangers.

It was after I closed the closet door that I turned and noticed the big trunk at the foot of the bed.

I opened it and saw that it seemed to be a repository for family documents. I flipped through an album that showed Doug and her on their wedding day and photographs of their son, Mark, shortly after birth and at various stages of life thereafter. A happy-looking child, with her delicate features but his father's blond hair. I assessed his beanpole physique and wondered if his father had expected him to make the football team.

I saw him graduating from grammar school and I saw him on family picnics and playing catch with his dad. Each photo was carefully documented with a date and place, and I judged it was her handwriting, because some photos bore legends such as *Mark and Doug at the beach,* and *Mark and Doug with Mark's first buck.*

And then, two years ago, the pages went blank.

I closed the book with a sense of having invaded a private tragedy.

Under the album was a cardboard box, and against my better instincts, I opened it.

A welter of papers confronted me. As I flipped through them, I saw that they were mostly bank statements and receipts.

A four-year-old dunning letter to Doug Devlin from a local car dealer and stapled to it a thank-you from the same merchant for full payment of the outstanding debt of $5,719. A series of credit card bills, to the limit, and stapled to them a canceled check signed by Doug Devlin for the full sum of $6,024. A receipt for a Yamaha four-wheeled ATV for $3,040, marked PAID-CASH. And there were others, including a stack of bank statements and canceled checks, most signed by Doug Devlin. They seemed to span a period of three years, from almost four years before the present to the time of Doug's death.

I started down at them and slowly it came through to me why they were here: They were Cyn's attempt to make sense of her family's finances. I wondered if she had succeeded.

Then, under some clothes, my hand touched something else. A small envelope, yellowed now, with a stamped return address.

*Rev. Thomas Wilbur,*
*P.O. Box 75 Farmerville, LA 71241*

It was addressed in a slanted hand in blue ink, but it wasn't the handwriting that got my attention, it was the address:

*Cynthia J. Brown*
*No. 1764511*
*Louisiana Correctional Institute for Women*
*P. O. Box 26*
*St. Gabriel, Louisiana 70776*

I stared down at it for a long time, thinking if I blinked, the letters might resolve themselves into some other words. The postmark was barely legible, but I made out the last two digits of the year, 78.

I took a deep breath and slipped the note out of the envelope.

The ink was faded, but I could read it. Aside from the date at the top, it was only a couple of lines.

*Dear Cynthia Jane:*

*I know that this is a difficult time in your life but you must know that salvation lies in the Lord Jesus Christ and accepting Him. You will be in my prayers.*

*Sincerely,*
*Thomas Wilbur*

I stared at it for a long time. Cyn had told me she'd come from poverty, but she hadn't told me she'd been in prison. Maybe that explained her dislike for Staples. Maybe she felt that way about all lawmen. Or was it something else? Was she afraid he knew about her past, or, as bad, might find out?

From the date, it looked like she had been incarcerated just before she'd met her husband. I wondered if she'd told him or whether this was something she had locked away into the past and wanted to keep there.

But what could her crime have been? She hadn't stayed long, so it couldn't have been anything too terrible.

That only left a few hundred offenses, from attempted murder to extortion.

I was replacing the paper in the envelope when I heard the car returning. I thrust the note back down into the trunk, put the box of receipts and the album over it, and then closed the trunk lid and flipped off the light switch.

The door downstairs opened, and I tiptoed back to the bedroom at the end of the hall and slipped out of my pants. Then her steps sounded on the stairs and her door closed softly.

But I'd had a chance to look at my watch before I'd left her room, and the luminous dial showed she'd been gone only forty-five minutes, not nearly enough time to make it to Baton Rouge and back.

Meg was safe, and I was going to look like a fool in the morning.

I told myself I should feel relieved. The woman who was sleeping across the hall wasn't a murderess.

But that was scant solace. For if she wasn't a murderess, what was she?

# ▬ SIXTEEN

I slept badly the rest of the night and finally roused myself when dawn began to lighten the texture of the darkness. I lay in bed a long time trying to put things together. Cyn had been in prison, though for what I didn't know. She'd fled to a marriage with someone who wanted her for her good looks, and she'd been too young to ask many questions. Then she'd found that marriage wasn't the answer to her troubles. Life had started to collapse around her again, first with the death of her son and then of her husband. And her husband's demise seemed to be linked to some strange source of income that she had been trying to fathom, judging from the documents in the box.

But what source of income?

Then I remembered what Meg had told me in the hospital room yesterday and wondered why I hadn't thought about it before.

*The storekeeper was busy talking to the mailman when we got there. He asked us what we were doing, and David said we were archaeologists. Somebody asked us if we were looking for Lee Oswald's buried treasure and everybody laughed.*

Was that it? Lee Oswald's buried treasure?

My skin began to go cold, and then I felt myself trembling. The implications were something I didn't want to confront. *Oswald's treasure.* Oswald had never had any money. All his short life he had bounced from one job to the other. Even his Marine Corps duty had been cut short by his request for a hardship discharge. It was all in the Warren Report, next to my bed at home.

Stories of treasure always sprang up around desperadoes. I could name a half-dozen communities in Louisiana that had buried loot from Jesse James, Lafitte the pirate, or, in the case of central Louisiana, the West-Kimbrel gang. There was the story of the lost Spanish gold in the Livingston Parish swamp and countless lost steamships with Confederate bullion. It would be natural—even inevitable—for such a rumor to spring up around a man who had committed what some considered the crime of the century.

Unless . . .

I got up and went to stand by the window, arms across my chest to keep from shaking.

Was it possible? I remembered what Clyde Fontenot had said the last time I'd talked to him. I'd written him off as a crazy man, but now . . .

"Alan."

I turned my head to see her looking through the partly open door, fully dressed.

"I heard you moving," she said. "You're up early."

"Just a bad habit," I said, suddenly aware that I was in my shorts. "Like taking long drives at one o'clock."

"I couldn't sleep," she said. "I went for a drive. I do that sometimes. I can't explain. It's just this feeling of being cooped up, the need to—well—assert my freedom."

*Prison*, I thought, but said nothing.

"But last night it was something else," she went on. "I had to think."

I waited.

"I'd been around before I met Doug. He wasn't the first man for me or the second or third. Knowing that drove him crazy. But at the same time he liked what I knew how to do. Sometimes I felt like I was just his whore. And sometimes he treated me like that. It's not a part of my life I like to dwell on, and I thought I was pretty much past that, doing things on impulse. I liked to believe that these days I was cool and collected and planned every move. But last night I was willing to forget everything."

"What's the crime? Being human? That your life isn't over because you're widowed?"

"I know, I've been through all that. It's probably my upbringing. My mother was religious. I often wondered if that was what drove my father to drink, all that piety. I spent Wednesday night in church and most of Sunday. I grew up with a healthy sense of sin, or maybe unhealthy. I rebelled against it, of course, but it's still there."

"Well, we've all got a lot of excess baggage," I said.

"Yes." She gave a wistful smile.

I turned around and reached for my pants. She gave a little gasp.

"What are those marks on your leg?"

I looked down at my calf and laughed.

"I got into an ant nest last year. The marks take a while to go away."

"That's not an ant bite," she said, pointing to the dead-white swath on my ankle.

"No. That's a burn. I caught on fire once. In Mexico."

Her fingers reached out to trace the dead flesh and then drew back.

"It doesn't hurt?"

"It did then. Now it only itches sometimes." I shrugged. "Face it, you're looking at a beat-up old archaeologist, or what's left of him."

My skin was tingling where she'd touched me, and she must have been able to tell, because she turned quickly and walked out of the room. I knew the temptation was past. For now.


We had breakfast and then she took me to the hospital. We circled the lot until I saw David's Land Rover, and then she took me to the door.

"I guess this is it," she said.

"For now," I replied.

I got out quickly and walked in through the automatic doors, past a statue of the sad-faced Virgin.

I found David stretched between two chairs in Meg's room. He roused himself as I came in and rubbed his eyes.

"Did I do good?" he asked sarcastically. "I chased out

a nun, two attendants, and somebody looking for Uncle Elmer.''

"You did good," I said.

"Think it's time to tell me what the hell this is all about?''

I saw Meg stirring and motioned him to come outside.

In the hall I told him what had happened.

"I just couldn't take a chance," I said.

"Well, we all have to do our part."

I stared past him. "I owe you one. Thanks."

"Bullshit," he snorted. "You owe me ten or twenty."

We made it to the field by eight-thirty, not too bad, except that in three hours the sun would be scalding down like a hot poker. We'd picked up another hand, this one the business major. I gave him about half a day, but what the hell? We were short of people and he deserved a chance. I just hoped we didn't have to carry him home.

I took over the crew until noon, giving David the easier job of finishing up work at the site we'd found. Halfway along I told myself I was too old for this sort of work. When I stepped on the hornet nest I decided *anybody* was too old for this.

I got away with just a couple of stings and stood there sweating. In my imagination I heard Bombast's voice.

*You mean this transect was not linear? The government is paying for linear transects . . .*

I mumbled a curse at Bombast and made my way around a berry patch.

I dropped my shovel and screen and stopped to wipe the sweat out of my eyes. Below me was the creek, fresh and cool. I had an urge to abandon my tools and stumble down to the sands and lie in the cold waters, letting them cleanse me of the perspiration and dirt.

As I watched, I suddenly found myself wondering if the man who had shot Kennedy had gazed down on the same view and had the same desire.

Or had he been looking out over the terrain for another purpose, searching for the right place to hide something, something he had been given in payment for an act too terrible to name?

If so, who had given him the money? They would all be dead now, wouldn't they?

By noon I'd managed to survey another hundred and fifty yards and made my way back to the staging point.

A few minutes later David showed up with some bags of artifacts from the site and brought out the cooler with his lunch.

After lunch I left David in charge and took the Land Rover into town.

I was looking for Clyde Fontenot, who seemed to think he had the answers, but his wife said he was out and she didn't know when he'd return. Instead I dropped by the post office and found Adolph Dewey working on a ham sandwich and a bottle of orange pop.

"You look like hell," he chuckled. "Found anything?"

"A few hornets," I said.

"Got to watch those berry patches. By the way, how they looking? Ripe yet?"

"Just about," I said.

"God, I love a berry pie," Dewey said. "You like black-berries?"

"My mother used to make cobblers," I said. "We'd go out picking in early June. What she didn't use for the cobbler she'd put in jars."

"The old people knew how to do it," he lamented. "My wife does okay. But not like her mother. Though I wouldn't tell her that."

"Speaking of the old-timers," I said, "who were the political powers in this parish thirty-five years ago?"

Dewey squinted and wiped his mouth with a napkin.

"Thirty-five years ago? Well . . ." He suppressed a belch. "There was the sheriff, Ryan Bilbo. Finally got him-self indicted for vote fraud and spent a year in one of them federal country clubs, three, four years back. I was a deputy then. There was Judge Persons. He handled this whole dis-trict. Tough man, the judge. He's been gone since about '75. Strong states' rights man. Ran for governor once, al-most got elected. There was the D.A., P. O. Martin. But he mainly did what the others wanted. And there was two or three who weren't elected to anything, just pulled the strings of them that was. Old man McNair tried to buy the whole damn parish. Owned half those gravel pits on the Amite. Got himself killed in an airplane crash in the early sixties. Shadwell Grimes owned the bank. But he didn't get involved in much that didn't affect him personally. Still, you wouldn't have wanted to cross the bastard. Died going over his books after they passed the inter-parish banking law back in '84. And then, of course, there was Timothy Devlin.''

"Timothy Devlin?"

"Oh, yeah. He had land and he had money, and that made him somebody to listen to, at least around here. And God but he hated a nigger.''

"Did he?" I said.

"You better believe. 'Course, lots of folks up here don't have much use for niggers, but with old Timothy it was damn near a crusade. Wouldn't even have 'em around to mow the lawn. Said they was all shiftless and thieves.'' He shrugged. "Well, you know what I mean.''

"Was he Klan?"

"Klan, White Gentlemen, White Citizens' Council, you name it. There wasn't anything halfway about old Timothy.''

I thought of the grizzled face in the little picture beside Blake Curtin's bed.

"John Birch Society?" I asked.

Another chuckle. "Seems to me he was in that, too. Always screaming how the politicians were selling out the country. Had one of them bumper stickers, 'Impeach Earl Warren.' Always passing out petitions. Got a lot of signers, too.''

"How did he feel about the Kennedys?"

Dewey emitted a guffaw.

"They were Satan hisself. I never seen old Timothy so close to a stroke as when somebody said something good about JFK after the missile business. Said John Kennedy was just the spoiled son of a bootlegger, that he was ruining our way of life, and his brother was just like him. It was Roosevelt all over again.''

"Anything else?"

"Well . . ." Dewey wadded up his napkin and threw it into a trash can. "You gotta understand, talk's cheap and in those days the idea of somebody actually killing the president was more like science fiction."

I waited.

"Lotsa people wished Jack Kennedy would drop dead. He made a lot of people down here mad."

"What did Timothy say?"

"Like I told you, he was always sounding off about something or other, so people didn't take him very serious. But he did say it at least in my hearing once."

He traced a pattern in the moisture ring the orange pop had left on the counter and then looked up at me.

"What?" I demanded. "What did Timothy say?"

Adolph Dewey gave a crooked little grin, and I saw that one of his lower incisors was gold. "He said, 'I wish somebody would kill the son-of-a-bitch and put this country back on the right track.' "

# ≡ SEVENTEEN

I stared at him.

"Do you remember when?"

The assistant postmaster shrugged. "I dunno. A year before Kennedy was killed. Or a few months. More likely a year, because he never said nothing more about it afterward and I didn't remember it until a good time after the assassination. I think he knew he'd shot off his mouth too much and he didn't want people coming around asking questions. After that old Timothy just laid low."

*Timothy Devlin. A virulent states' rightser and hatemonger. A man with more than enough money to pay an assassin . . .*

"You look kinda weak," Dewey said. "You had a little too much sun, fella?"

I took a deep breath.

"I'll be okay."

"You wanna sit there 'til you get your strength back?"

"I'm fine. Thanks, Mr. Dewey."

"You ain't seen any ghosts out there on the old place, have you? Lee Harvey, for instance?" He laughed loudly, and I managed to shake my head. "Well, keep a lookout."

I made my way back out into the sun and got into the Land Rover. The atmosphere was stifling. Reality swam like a mirage in front of my eyes.

We had gone berry picking every year at a patch just outside of town on the river road, and my mother had made sweet cobblers with homemade dough. Before Lee Oswald had come to Jackson, Louisiana, looking for work at the hospital.

Except that now I wondered. Had it just been a ruse? A lie to cover the actual reason he had *really* come here one August day? Had he come because powerful men in New Orleans knew someone here who'd be willing to pay for a job only an Oswald would do? Had they listened to Oswald brag at French Quarter parties about his marksmanship in the Marines and the rifle he had bought from a mail-order house and how he could change the course of history if given the right chance? Had they known about Timothy Devlin and his hatreds, known that he would put up the money to hire the sick young man with a craving for fame?

There were details missing, of course. Somebody had to have known several months ahead of time that Kennedy would be in Dallas that day, and the official story was that the trip hadn't been planned that far in advance. The motorcade route hadn't been published until four days before Kennedy's arrival. But there had always been rumors about someone high in the administration who had been a part of the plot.

Was I going crazy? It was too strange to believe. Above all, I didn't *want* to believe it.

But it had a terrible plausibility, and there were people who had seen Oswald here.

I thought about the receipts in the trunk in Cyn's bedroom. Old Timothy had given Oswald a down payment, and Oswald had buried it somewhere on the property. Then Oswald had been killed. The money had stayed there until years later, when Timothy's son had found it and used it to pay off his debts. And then had been killed himself, either by accident or by someone else looking for the money. Cyn had figured part of it out, enough to know her husband, once desperate for money, had found the stash and spent only a fraction of it by the time of his death.

Another terrible thought came to me then. Was that why she was opposed to selling even Buck's land? Was she convinced the cache lay somewhere in those woods and that selling the land would cheat her of the chance to find it? Was Buck, then, the only one of the family who was completely innocent of what had happened? Buck, the professional military man, who could probably kill with a piano wire or a knife?

I drove into Clinton and stopped at the courthouse, where I found Esmerelda in the clerk's office, engrossed in the conveyance books.

"So did you fight back?" she asked when she saw me.

"Against what?"

"The bear that left you for dead."

"Very funny."

Esmerelda closed her legal pad and shoved her glasses further up on her thin nose.

"Not trying to be. David says you've been acting funny lately. Aunt Esme is here to listen."

I managed a smile. Esmerelda was everybody's aunt. A widow who had gone back to school ten years ago and earned a doctorate in Southern History, she was a denizen of the conveyance books and tax records, and seemingly only came up for air to look bored in times between work.

I glanced around the room, but the only other person was a sleepy-looking clerk near the front.

"What have you found about Timothy Devlin?" I asked.

"Timothy Devlin?" She stared at me through her lenses like I'd asked about the dead czar. "Nothing. He isn't in here. Why?"

"Isn't in there?"

"No. The Devlin property is on the west side of Thompson Creek. That's West Feliciana Parish. I haven't made it to the St. Francisville courthouse yet."

I hit the counter with the flat of my hand.

"Score one for you."

"You need to know something about him?" she asked, peering at me.

"I want whatever you turn up. He died in 1980. I'd like to know what of."

She nodded. "That's easy enough. But why do you want to know? Is this one of your wild-goose chases? This have something to do with Meg?"

"Meg? Why should it?"

"Because I know you, Alan. You've got something in

your teeth and you're running away with it."

"Well, maybe. Just check for me, will you?"

"Sure. I'll do it tomorrow."

"Thanks, Esme."

"You won't thank me when you get my bill."

I went back to the survey area and, instead of waiting for the others, walked down to the creek and then up again to the cabin.

Had Oswald really come here, then? And had he buried his assassin's fee somewhere nearby?

But why here? Why not take it back to New Orleans with him? Why bury it on someone else's property when he couldn't even drive an automobile and would have had to make special arrangements to come up here and get it? When someone else who knew the land might find it first?

Or had he fallen in with somebody already here, someone who had put the notion in his head?

Doug Devlin?

I thought of the woman in the big house, with her own demons to battle. Had she suspected her husband of complicity in the Oswald affair? Any connection with Oswald would have been before they met, when Doug was very young, a teenager. A teenager under the sway of a powerful, domineering father . . .

I went back down to the creek, stooping to scoop up some water and splash it over myself, washing away some of the sweat and dirt. But I knew it would take more than water to wash away the other kind of dirt I felt.

We packed up and half an hour later were in Baton Rouge. I went straight home, not bothering to check for messages at the office, and submerged myself in the tub. When I had sponged off the last of the grime, I dried, dressed, and drove out to the hospital to see Meg.

A stern-looking man with thinning hair was standing by her bed with a dumpy blond woman who looked up at me in alarm.

"Oh, Alan. I want you to meet my parents."

Mr. Lawrence gave me his hand in slow motion, and Mrs. Lawrence tried to smile.

"We flew here as soon as I could get away," Meg's

father said. "Are you the person responsible?"

I gulped. "I'm the owner of the company."

"You're the one who left her to work alone in that building," he accused.

"Now, Norman," the wife said, but Norman was only getting up steam.

"Don't you have any sense of responsibility?" he demanded.

"Daddy," Meg remonstrated, "it was my idea. Alan didn't have anything to do with it."

"You just listen, Margaret," her father commanded. "It's his responsibility to take reasonable care."

I felt queasy. Norman Lawrence talked like a lawyer.

"Mr. Lawrence, we have an alarm system and it functioned. Nobody could have foreseen what happened. But I do feel responsible, because I like Meg and she's doing a good job, and if there's anything at all . . ."

"What you can do, Mr. Graham, is find another employee, because this one doesn't work for you anymore. And you might talk to your attorney in the morning, if you haven't already."

"Daddy!" We all turned to the tiny figure in the bed. "If you don't stop that, I'll get up and walk out of here right now. They're going to discharge me in the morning, but I feel well enough to walk this minute, and I will. I'll go stay with a friend. And if you try to sue Alan, I swear you'll never see me again!"

Norman Lawrence's mouth opened, and his wife grabbed his arm.

"Norman, she means it."

"You're damned right I do," Meg shouted, and her father flinched like somebody had slapped him. "Alan hasn't been anything but nice to me, and what happened isn't his fault. If you were any kind of father at all, you'd be helping him get to the bottom of it instead of standing here making threats. What kind of a lawyer are you, anyway?"

Lawrence coughed and looked from his wife to me.

"I'll leave you folks with your daughter," I said and stepped into the hall.

I went home and checked my answering machine. The

only message was from Marilyn, telling me the locksmith had fixed the broken door and the alarm was functioning again. She also mentioned that two new floodlights had been installed, one in front and one in back, and she hoped we'd get some use out of them before the utility company cut off our service for nonpayment. I thought of calling Cyn, restrained myself, then gave in and called anyway. The phone rang five times, six, seven, and finally I gave up.

The house seemed lonelier than ever after the family scene I'd just witnessed. There had been yelling and threats, but they had all arisen from love.

I left quickly and went to the office. It was just growing dark, but the floodlight already lent an unreal air, as if I were entering a movie set. I unlocked the front door, punched in the code to deactivate the alarm, and locked the door behind me.

Everything seemed to be in order. I didn't know why I was there, except that I didn't want to be at home. I went to my desk and saw a pink message slip with Marilyn's handwriting:

*Call Mr. Fontenot.*

On the slip was his telephone number. I started to dial, then thought I might be taking him from supper. I'd be up there tomorrow, anyway, so I'd make it a point to drop by again. What I wanted to talk to him about was better said in person.

I went back out to the sorting table and looked at the trays. A new pile of potsherds had been brought in, and I went through them in a desultory fashion, noting some with ground-up shell as temper and others with hatchwork designs engraved on the clay after firing. A late assemblage, likely from somewhere near the mouth of the Red River. I was still contemplating them when the phone rang.

I picked it up.

"Alan?" It was Cyn's voice, throaty and strong, as if she were in the next room.

"Where are you?" I asked.

"At home. Look, did you call earlier?"

"Twenty minutes ago."

"God," she breathed, "it really *was* you."

"You were there?"

"Don't get mad, but I heard it ring, and I thought, *What if it's him?* I wanted to talk to you so much. Then I thought, *What if it isn't him?* I couldn't stand finding out it was somebody else, that you hadn't called at all. Pretty stupid, huh?"

"So finally *you* decided to make the call," I said.

She sighed. "Well, I just wanted to tell you that you left something here."

"What?"

"Give me a while to invent something. Oh, damn, Alan, I'm so messed up. I keep thinking about last night and I feel so stupid . . ."

"Don't."

"Can't we just start over again?"

"No need. It's okay, really."

"I don't guess you had any plans to come up this way."

But before I answered, the little envelope with the note from a minister intruded:

*Dear Cynthia Jane:*

*I know that this is a difficult time in your life . . .*

And that wasn't the only thing I needed to ask her. There was much more. I needed to ask her about old Timothy and about her husband. I needed to ask her if Doug had ever said anything about a young man with a smirk who appeared one day from nowhere and asked to see Doug's father. I needed to know if Cyn Devlin, formerly Cynthia Jane Brown of the Louisiana Correctional Institute for Women, had found out about a payment made to the young man with a smirk and had traced it through her husband's business dealings. And most of all, I had to know whether the man someone had found lying on the sand last year had been killed by the woman he had taken out of poverty.

How do you ask a woman if she's a killer and if those

close to her have conspired in one of the worst crimes of the century?

"I didn't have any plans to do anything," I said. "I'm pretty tired."

"Sure." There was fatalism in her tone.

"Look, Cyn . . ."

"What?"

"Nothing. I'll call you soon."

"Yeah. Good night."

"Good night." I hung up, overcome by feelings of helplessness. I sat there for a long time, and it was only when the dusk had changed to full darkness that I realized the little light on the answering machine was blinking.

Without thinking, I pressed the Replay button.

La Bombast's voice whined forth in all its mechanical authority:

"Alan, this is Bertha Bomberg. I have some time free tomorrow and I've decided to drive up. I want to see the progress of the survey. Don't do anything special. And I mean it. I just want to see an ordinary day in the field. You can expect me at your office at eight. Please don't leave before I get there. Goodbye."

I got up slowly, feeling drained. How much more good news could I take in one day?

# ▰Eighteen

It was quarter to nine when the white Corps of Engineers car nosed into the curb across from my office. The crew, which had been milling around for the better part of an hour, looked at one another, then at the car. The driver's door opened, and La Bombast dismounted.

Square-jawed and big-boned, with close-cropped black hair, she wasn't bad looking if you'd been at sea for three years. Or if you liked ice sculpture.

"You really need a parking lot," she said. "Like Pyramid."

"Then why didn't you people give Pyramid a contract last go-round?" I shot back without thinking.

"I'm sure they'll reapply," she said with a smile that dripped venom. She looked around at the crew.

"Are all these people waiting on me? You don't have any lab work they could be doing?"

David spoke then. "They were expecting to leave at eight."

"So was I. I was up at six. But things happen. I won't bother to try to explain." She was in her field clothes, pants that were a size too small for her ample hips and a safari shirt that screamed Banana Republic. "Now, should I ride with you?"

"Please do," I said drily.

I waited until we were out of the city traffic to speak. "There's a landowner problem," I told her.

"You didn't mention that."

118

I shrugged. It was true that Cyn had agreed to let us pass, but I didn't want to be in her debt until I could resolve the doubts that were plaguing my mind.

"We're almost finished on the west side," I said.

"Well, I want to see the site."

I thought about the progress we'd hoped to make on the survey today. It would be better to get as much done as we could before the sun began to beat the crew down. And they'd be nervous as long as La Bombast was around.

"I thought I'd take you over to visit with Esmerelda at the West Feliciana courthouse," I said. "Let you see what she's finding about land ownership, then get a good lunch, and come back this afternoon and show you the site."

Bertha gave me a doubting look.

"I really ought to . . ."

"And we need to clear a trail. There're so many briars. Esme said there's a good little place to get chicken-fried steaks . . ."

I was hoping I'd remembered her food preferences correctly.

"Well, if you think . . ."

"It'll be an easier walk when we come back."

"Alan, you're not doing a number?"

"Bertha!"

There had to be a greasy spoon in St. Francisville that served chicken-fried steaks.

It took us thirty minutes to make the trip west to St. Francisville, a town two centuries old that perches on the bluffs overlooking the Mississippi and watches the river traffic come and go. The homes are antebellum and gracious, and the shops along Main Street testify to the power of the tourist industry. The plantations around it have names like Roselawn, the Myrtles, and Afton Villa.

We parked in front of the courthouse, an ancient Gothic structure shaded by live oaks, and went in.

Esme was in the clerk's office, her nose buried in a conveyance book.

She looked up and did a good job of hiding her surprise.

"Hello, Bertha. And Alan."

I wondered what I'd have to do to make it up to her.

For the next half-hour Esmerelda patiently showed Bertha her notes and explained the chains of title for the two tracts. Bertha listened and asked some surprisingly cogent questions. I knew she respected Esmerelda both as a historian and a sister in arms.

Afterward I steered Bertha to the old Episcopalian cemetery across the street where she wandered happily among the graves, snapping pictures.

I excused myself to go back across the street, to use the facilities, but sought out Esme instead.

"Alan—" she began.

"I'm sorry. I'll buy you lunch. Is there a place around here that serves chicken-fried steaks?"

Esme made a face. "I hope not."

"What about old Timothy Devlin? Have you found anything out about him?"

"Him and his son both." She waved some photocopies. "I have the probate records."

My heart started to race.

"And?"

She shrugged. "Old Timothy owned a lot of land in this parish and some in Mississippi. I'd put his worth at about two and a half million when he died."

*Two million.* How much would have been required to kill a president thirty-six years ago? A hundred thousand? A quarter of a million? A half?

"Look, Esme, did you find anything indicating he sold a lot of his land in 1963? Anything that showed he might have needed ready cash?"

Esme leaned on the counter, staring down her angular nose at me.

"Old Timothy Devlin was *always* buying and selling land. I didn't see any pattern, but I wasn't looking for any. You wanna tell me what this is about?"

"I'm not sure."

"Well, you'd do better to look at his bank records for that time. Now his son, there's not any mystery there."

"Oh?"

"He was selling everything he could get his grubby little hands on from the day they put Timothy in the ground. The estate was divided between the two sons, and Douglas blew his in a few years. He even mortgaged the old home at one point, and it almost went at a sheriff's sale.''

"And?"

It was her turn to shrug.

"On the day the mortgage came due, Douglas paid it off in cash. Two hundred and fifty-three thousand smackers.''

I blinked.

"Thanks, Esme."

It all held together: the payoff to the assassin, the hiding of the money, then Douglas's finding it later and using it to save himself. I thought of Clyde Fontenot and his strange machine.

It was a metal detector—I'd used them enough to know one when I saw it. But he'd had it hooked to a car battery, which made me believe he was trying to boost the power. So it wasn't Oswald's ghost Clyde Fontenot was concerned about, it was something more tangible. All the talk of ghost hunting was a convenient camouflage, because no one worried about a crazy man.

I thought of the pink message slip then.

*Call Mr. Fontenot.*

We ate at a place on Highway 61, just south of town, where the assistant clerk of court told me they served steaks the way Bertha liked. La Bombast seemed satisfied, cutting her meat into tiny portions as if it might go further that way. When we were done, I told Esmerelda goodbye, and we drove back over toward Jackson. But instead of heading up the narrower blacktop to the survey area, I kept going east. Bertha said nothing, perhaps because she was sated. Or maybe, I thought, she didn't know the roads well enough. I turned into the Fontenot yard and went to the door.

There was nobody home.

I thought of walking around to the back, but there were no vehicles in the drive, so I gave up.

"What was that all about?" Bertha asked.

"An informant on local history," I said.

"Oh. I'm glad you're using them."

"We try," I said.

It was not quite two o'clock when we got out at the staging area.

Bertha squinted up at the glaring sun, started to say something, and thought better of it.

"I'll take you over to the site now," I told her, clipping my canteen to my belt.

She grabbed her safari hat out of the Blazer and stuck it down over her head. We headed downhill and when we got to the creek, I splashed through the water, then turned around on the sandbar.

"It's not deep," I said, calculating that it was just deep enough to drown her half boots.

Her mouth tightened, and then she followed, splashing like a water buffalo. I stopped on the other side and waited. But when she reached the bank, she kept going.

"Come on."

She was taking it as a duel.

We reached the top of the hill, and she started for the woods and the cabin, but I pointed to my right.

"This way."

We started along what was now a fairly well-marked path through the brush.

"I thought you had somebody clear this today," she accused.

"They were supposed to."

Ten minutes later we reached the site, and I set about explaining exactly what we had found and where. She listened intently, asked questions, and seemed reasonably satisfied. From somewhere in the distance I heard a shout and knew the crew was at work.

I unfastened my canteen and held it out to her.

"Water?"

"No. Thanks."

I shrugged and took a long drink.

"Cold, just like it ought to be," I said.

Her eyes darted to the canteen and she licked her lips.

"You sure?" I asked, thrusting the canteen her way again.

"I'm fine."

I hooked the canteen back over my belt, and she started

down the trail ahead of me. I caught her stopping several times to wipe the perspiration from her face and smiled grimly, then chastised myself for my thoughts. After all, the last thing I needed was for her to have heatstroke. It would be a logistical nightmare to drag her out.

It was three-thirty when we reached the place where the trail led up to the cabin. This time when I held out the canteen she accepted, though she was careful not to take more than a couple of gulps.

"So where did this murder you told me about take place?" she asked.

I smiled. So she was human after all.

"Right down there," I said, pointing to the creek. "In fact, from what I'm told, we passed the spot."

I explained how Doug Devlin had been found sprawled on the sand, just on the East Feliciana side, with his feet still in the water.

"Well, maybe his wife did it," she said, and I felt a stirring of anxiety. "Most violence is in the family."

"Yes."

All at once I wanted to get away from here, get across the stream and up on the other side, to the vehicles.

But Bertha was clearly intrigued. "It was a while ago, you said?"

"Last year," I told her.

She started to pick her way downhill.

"I don't see why they couldn't have found the person that did it. Especially with modern technology."

"I don't know," I said, as she reached the bottom.

"They probably don't have a scientific laboratory in these rural communities," she opined.

"I think that's a safe bet."

She bent over to scoop up water with her hand, but most of the water leaked out.

"I'm going down here where it's deeper," she said, pointing upstream.

"Bertha, I'd be careful—"

"I can swim, for God's sake." She started across the sandbar toward a deeper pool in the distance.

"I've heard there's quicksand," I said, following.

"That's ridiculous." She reached the end of the bar and, to my surprise, stepped down into the water. I saw it rise to her calves.

"Bertha, there are holes. You could step into one that's over your head."

She turned to fix me with a glare.

"I'm the government," she said.

I shrugged and watched her splash forward, the water rising up toward her waist.

"This is wonderful," she said.

Little alarm bells were going off now, but mainly because she had stopped in her tracks, as if something was wrong.

"What's that over there?" she asked, her voice suddenly shaky.

I looked past her to some bushes on the west side. Some red-colored cloth seemed to be caught in them, floating on the surface like an old laundry bag.

"Alan . . ."

I waded toward her, and when I glimpsed her face I saw it was ashen.

"What's that?" she demanded.

"Stay here," I said and started toward the far bank.

The water was to my waist now, and I could feel the stirrings of a current. It was the current that had brought the laundry bag here and nested it against the cut bank in the bushes.

Except that now I could see that it was no laundry bag, and my stomach began to do flip-flops.

I came up to the bank, the water receding to my knees, then my calves. I didn't want to keep going, because I could see now what it was, and it wasn't a laundry bag, as I'd hoped, but something else.

"Alan!"

I ignored her cry, my eyes fixed on the object under the bushes.

It was a human body, male, judging from the shortness of the hair. He was dressed in a long-sleeved red shirt and a pair of blue jeans. The ears projected from the head like flags.

I stared down, not wanting to touch him, knowing what I would find. Little ripples from my steps were still lapping at him, making him rise and fall in the water like a baby being rocked to sleep, and I thought for an instant that he might come loose from the bushes and float away.

*"Alan!"*

There was nothing else to be done. I reached down, grasped his shoulders, and turned him faceup. As I did, I stumbled in the water, and the body wrenched out of my grasp. As it floated downstream toward Bertha, I heard a shriek, and at the same time caught sight of the dead, fish-colored face.

It was a face I knew, one that in life had been intelligent but now was fixed in an expression of eternal surprise.

There was a third eye in Clyde Fontenot's face, where someone had shot him, and my guess from the look on his face was that he had known who it was.

# ≡ NINETEEN

Over the next three hours I gave three separate statements. The first was to Sheriff Staples, who made his way carefully down to the water's edge in his double-wing shoes and directed his deputies from there. The second was to a state policeman named Connell, who wrote quickly on a pad and told me I'd have to come in and sign my statement later. And the third was to Sheriff Buford Cooney of West Feliciana Parish, a gray-haired heavyweight in denims, who stomped across the sand in his cowboy boots, spat tobacco to punctuate his commands, and reminded me that our paths had crossed once before, at a Tunica burial site. It was Cooney who pointed out that the body had been found against the cut bank on the west side. He was countered by Staples, who made it clear that the body was now on the east side and that, in any case, the fact that it had nested against the cut bank only showed that the water ran faster on that side and that Fontenot might well have been killed on the east bank and fallen into the stream.

Cooney only spat more juice and skewered him with pig eyes.

The state policeman retreated tactfully, knowing enough not to be caught between two rural political bosses.

I was reminded of the situation after Doug Devlin had been shot: It was impossible to get any sort of coordinated investigation under the circumstances.

Bertha, in the meantime, had been assisted uphill, professing heat exhaustion. I'd had David drive her back to Baton Rouge with the rest of the crew.

By five o'clock the ambulance had taken away the body, and I went to Clinton to sign my statement for Staples and the state trooper. Cooney had growled that I was expected in St. Francisville tomorrow to do the same, and I nodded. While in the Clinton office I overheard one of the deputies saying that Mrs. Fontenot had last seen her husband leaving the house at dawn.

Maybe when I appeared in Cooney's office I could find out whether the lawman had known old Timothy Devlin.

Once I was done in Clinton, I drove back west, toward the survey area, but instead of turning north before Thompson Creek, I kept on straight and turned in at Cyn's.

I had to know where she was when it happened.

But her station wagon was gone, and my knocks on the door went unanswered. I went out to the road and checked her mailbox, but the little flag was down, and the box was empty, so someone must have picked up her mail.

I started back to town, feeling sapped.

I hadn't given my theory to the officials, but I thought I knew what had happened. Clyde Fontenot had gone hunting, but not for the ghost of an assassin, as he claimed. Instead, he had taken his homemade metal detector and gone searching for an assassin's fortune. But there had been someone else out there who had known about Oswald and who had his own designs on the money. He had shot Clyde, the same way they had killed Douglas Devlin last year.

The police report was wrong. Doug Devlin had been murdered, just as Clyde Fontenot had been murdered. They had been murdered because of something that had begun thirty-six years ago during a hot New Orleans summer. First there had been the schemers, and then their tool, Oswald, and finally there had been the man with money, Timothy Devlin.

I wondered how many others had also been involved.

Because men like Timothy move in packs. Hatred doesn't thrive by itself, it always attracts fellow haters. And in those days the Felicianas had been full of them. Rich white men with plantations, who saw blacks as little more than slave labor and resented anything the Kennedy administration might do to liberalize voting rights. They had been men of power, men of prestige, men of incredible arrogance. Men, I thought, like Sheriff Buford Cooney.

Of course, Cooney would have been young then, maybe thirty, and not a political boss yet, but he may have known. If not at the time, then later.

*Sheriff Cooney, I got some information for you. Something big. You just got to help me out now . . .*

I knew enough about Louisiana to know that was the way it went, all the way up to the governor's mansion.

The trouble was that there wasn't any way I was going to get Cooney to tell me.

And did it really matter? Timothy was gone. Anyone he had brought into the scheme was probably gone. Clay Shaw and David Ferrie and the rest of the New Orleans crowd that D.A. Jim Garrison had linked to Oswald were gone. Even Garrison was gone. The only one who was left, who had been close to Timothy and Doug, was a man too addled to speak.

But he hadn't always been addled. Once, Blake Curtin had been able to use his tongue. Once, when he had gone deer hunting with old Timothy and his son . . .

Something nudged at my consciousness, but I couldn't force it free. Something about Blake Curtin in his marine field jacket . . .

When I reached the office only David was there, with what remained of a six-pack of dark beer in front of him and his feet up on the sorting table. He hadn't changed from his field clothes and he looked as haggard as I felt. I saw an empty six-pack on the floor next to him.

"I figured you'd be in sooner or later," he said and shoved a beer into my hand.

"I had to sign some papers," I explained.

"Right." He swigged his beer and then slammed it down onto the table so that the artifacts in the sorting trays jumped. "Well, Bombast's gone back."

"And?"

"She's stopping work."

"What?" I'd been afraid that might happen.

"That's right. She says she's writing a Stop Work order tomorrow. Says it's too dangerous out there, says it's a crime scene and until this is all cleared up, it exposes the government to too much liability."

"Shit."

"That's what I said. Well, maybe she'll wreck on the way back to New Orleans."

I twisted off the cap and took a long pull of the bitter brew.

"Remember when I started working here?" David asked. I nodded.

"Seven years ago. I was a senior in college. My family thought I was crazy. First I drop my rabbinical studies, I go into religious studies here at LSU, then I get interested in the anthropological study of religion and switch over, and then I end up in archaeology. Took me six years to get my degree."

"You were always pretty slow," I said wryly.

"I remember the first job you ever gave me. You sent me out with a crew to the damndest swamp I ever saw. I had to make a transect through water halfway to my balls. I stepped on two snakes and gave every mosquito in the state a blood sample. We got to this little island and nobody could find the surveying flags, and we didn't know if we were on course or if we'd lost the path somewhere back there in the swamp."

"Rough one," I said.

He nodded.

"That was when I knew this was what I wanted to do."

I had a memory of a mud-smeared face with hollow eyes, not too unlike the one that now confronted me. He'd gone on to graduate school for his master's degree, and when he finished two years later, I'd taken him in as a full-fledged project manager.

"The bitch is that I still want to do it," he said.

I nodded.

"So you want to tell me what's going on?" he asked.

I shrugged and related my suspicions.

"And I thought you were against conspiracy theories," he said.

"I was. But there seems to be some good evidence here."

"What about the woman?"

A wave of nausea passed through me. Maybe I'd had too much sun. "I don't know."

"Is there something between you?"

"Ask me next week."

"Well, maybe Bombast will relent," he said. "Maybe they'll solve the murder. Maybe . . ."

"Yeah."

He tossed his empty bottle into the trash. "You know, even if it's true about Oswald, nobody'll ever believe it. It's been too long. The case is closed."

"I know."

I got up slowly, feeling every bone in my body complain.

"Go home," I said. "Get some rest. By the way, anybody check on Meg?"

"She's gone," David said. "I meant to tell you, but I didn't want to depress you anymore."

"*Gone?*" I spun to face him.

"Checked out with her parents. Said they were going back to Maryland. I heard her old man was royally pissed. He doesn't want her down here in yahoo land anymore."

"Christ."

Suddenly it seemed almost too much effort to move. At last I drifted out to the Blazer and sat in it a long time, only vaguely aware of the cars passing on the street. I made myself insert the key and start the engine, and only when I had the air conditioner blowing in my face did I come halfway to myself. I felt better after a shower, but not by that much.

It was the stress, of course. It always knocked the wind out of me at first, but in the past I'd always managed to catch my second wind.

Like the day I'd fought Ernie Slagle in the fourth grade. He'd ground my face into the dust and twisted my arm behind my back and he kept yelling something, taunting me.

And when I couldn't stand it anymore I'd found a source of energy I didn't know I had and rolled over, spilling him into the dirt. And when I drove my fist into his face and felt his nose crack, I'd had the satisfaction of seeing the surprise in his eyes.

Afterward neither of us would tell the principal what it was about, and I'd blocked most of the episode from my memory, except for bits and pieces.

But suddenly, alone now in the old house, thinking back to that terrible fall of 1963, when a man named Oswald had changed our lives, I remembered. And most of all I remembered what Ernie Slagle had been screaming.

I was standing in the middle of the living room, trembling, staring at the painting on the wall, the one I had grown up with, when the door chimes shook me out of it.

Cyn. It had to be. She'd heard what had happened and come here.

And yet even as I reached for the doorknob, I pulled my hand back.

So what would I tell her? I'd found a name for my own bogies and now I wanted to hear about hers?

The chimes sounded again, and I opened the door.

"Dr. Graham?"

There was a man standing on my porch, and it took me a while to recognize him. When I did, I cringed inwardly.

Because the man in front of me was the man who'd threatened to sue me only yesterday, the man who'd killed me with his eyes and taken his daughter out of my clutches.

Norman Lawrence, Meg's father.

# ■ TWENTY

"May I come in?" he asked.

I nodded and stepped back. He shut the door behind him, gave the room a cursory look, and then turned to face me.

"You know we're taking Meg back home with us."

"So I heard. In fact, I thought you were already gone."

"I felt it was best to get her out of the hospital, but we're staying in a motel. Her roommate will keep the apartment until the fall, when Meg comes back. But I'd like for some doctors at home to see her."

*The better to sue me with,* I thought.

"I understand. But Mr. Lawrence—"

He held up a hand, and his gold Rolex gleamed in the light.

"Let me finish. When Meg decided to come down here to school, her mother and I were naturally disappointed. She could have gone to any of a number of excellent schools in the area. Catholic University, William and Mary, even St. John's. But she claimed to want a change of scenery and she threatened to drop out entirely unless we sent her to Louisiana."

Which, I thought, had confirmed all his worst fears.

"She's been enrolled for a year now. Her grades are good, but frankly, we knew she wasn't getting the education she would have gotten at one of the better schools. Last year, when she took that field school business, I thought she'd get all this out of her system and come home, but instead she insisted on staying for the whole year. We held our breath through the entire school year, waiting for her to come back on vacation. Then she called and told us she was going to work for you this summer."

He folded his arms across his chest. I wondered if he wasn't hot in the coat and tie. But then I realized he probably didn't own any comfortable clothing.

"Naturally, Louise and I were disappointed. I suppose, to be honest, that I, at least, hoped she'd fail."

It was not an admission I'd expected to hear.

"She didn't," I told him quietly. "No matter what happened, she did an excellent job."

He nodded. "I guess she must have."

Norman Lawrence walked over to my mantel, picked up a small vase, turned it over in his hand, and then carefully set it back down.

"I suppose you know some of this is quite valuable." It was as if he were advising a client.

"Yes."

"In any case, when this happened to Meg, it just confirmed what I wanted to believe. You have to understand, sir, she's my only daughter."

"I think I understand," I said. "I was an only child."

"To have to leave everything, come down here, not knowing how badly hurt she was . . ." His chest slowly rose and fell. "Well, I imagine I was pretty impatient with you the other day."

"A little," I said.

"More than a little," he insisted. "After I got Meg out of the hospital, she let me have it with both barrels. Louise got involved, too. They let me know I was just one notch higher than Attila the Hun."

I felt some of the tension dissipate. He wasn't going to sue.

"Believe me, Mr. Lawrence, I'm as upset about this as you are." *And more,* I thought, *because today somebody was murdered over it.*

"I'm sure. Well . . ." He turned back to the door, suddenly at a loss. "I suppose I'd better get back to my family."

"Thank you for coming, Mr. Lawrence."

"I'm glad I did." He gave me his hand and we shook. Then, almost as an afterthought, he reached into his coat pocket. "By the way, here's my card. You can contact Meg through me if you don't have her address. And if there's anything I can do to help you, don't hesitate."

We shook hands again.

I watched him walk down the sidewalk and under the camphor trees to his car.

I glanced at his card:

*S. Norman Lawrence III, Assistant General Counsel, General Accounting Office, Washington, D.C.*

I put the card in my wallet and closed the door.

At least we wouldn't get sued, which was small comfort, since a defunct corporation, as my own lawyer once explained, has virtually no exposure. The beauty of the law.

It wasn't the law I was worried about now, though, it was my own demons.

The year had been 1963 and when I remembered that year, what usually came to mind was my father's ashen face and the stricken expression of my mother.

"The president was pronounced dead at 1 P.M. this afternoon at Parkland Hospital in Dallas."

My parents had cried and I had cried.

They were gone now, but the demons weren't.

If Pepper had been here I could have talked it out with her. My resentment boiled up, and I told myself I was being unreasonable.

"It's an unstable situation," she'd said. "I can't just move in with you, and I don't think either one of us is ready for marriage. We need time."

*We.*

I couldn't stay in this house tonight.

I dialed Cyn's number, but no one answered. Forty-five minutes later I was pulling into her drive, but her car was still gone. Blake Curtin's pickup was there, though, and there were lights on in the house. I got out and went around to the back, picking my way carefully in the darkness.

When I came to the back door I stopped. There was a sound of hammering inside. I went up the steps and peered through the glass of the back door. Blake Curtin was up on a ladder in the hallway, fastening a new duct cover for the central air.

I tried the door and it opened. I waited until he'd finished his job and then cleared my throat.

"Hello, Blake."

The man on the ladder jerked around, almost falling, and I went forward to steady his perch. For an instant his hand with the hammer hovered inches above my head, and then he started down slowly rung by rung.

"I'm sorry to startle you. I was looking for Mrs. Devlin."

Curtin frowned slightly and then shrugged.

"Have you seen her today?"

He shook his head *no*.

"Any idea where she is?"

He made a great circle motion with his left hand, and I took it he was saying she was far away.

I changed the subject. "Did you hear about what happened to Clyde Fontenot?"

Curtin stepped back suddenly, striking the wall with his back.

"Somebody killed him. He was found not very far from where Doug Devlin was found. Somebody shot him, too."

The handyman licked his lips, and his eyes hunted for an escape.

"Have you been here long? Has anybody else been here looking for Mrs. Devlin? Any policemen?"

He shook his head violently.

I could tell he was about to bolt, so I backed away.

"Well, sorry to bother you."

He gave a half nod, and I felt his eyes on my back as I went out the way I'd come. I backed out to the road, then saw the flag on the mailbox was still up. So no one had taken in today's delivery.

I sat beside the highway for a few minutes with my motor running, trying to think. But thoughts wouldn't come.

When I was small and the frustration had been more than I could live with, I'd once run away, legs pumping until there was no breath left. Now, thirty years later, I drove.

I went west to U.S. 61, then north through St. Francisville, Wakefield, and across the line into Mississippi. I rolled down my window and let the night air whip in and lick my face. The air was warm and smelled like the river half a mile to my left. I arrowed through Woodville and down through the Homochitto bottoms.

An hour and a half after I started, I was in Natchez and I stopped for a hamburger at a franchise place.

Maybe I was making this trip for nothing, but I couldn't just wait by myself, and I especially couldn't wait in the house on Park Boulevard.

After Natchez I stayed on 61, paralleling the Natchez Trace Parkway and slipping through Port Gibson and the other old antebellum river landings until I reached Vicksburg.

It was just after eleven, and there was still a small clot of Friday night traffic, mostly teenagers from across the river in Louisiana, but also a scatter of tourists here to see the Civil War battlefield.

What was it she'd told me?

*I couldn't sleep. I went for a drive. I do that sometimes.*

I crossed the river on the old bridge and was back in Louisiana. I could smell the heat rising up from the bean fields, and the memory of projects David and I had done over the years flashed through my mind. We'd dug into a temple mound just south of here, in Tensas Parish, and we'd excavated a prehistoric village near Tallulah in the squalid August heat. Lots of sweat, lots of memories.

After refueling in Monroe, I headed north on 165, into the hills.

It was one-thirty when I reached Farmerville, a tiny settlement that had once been a cotton and logging center. I was in the pinewoods now, and the fresh smell of ozone had taken the place of the hot, wet river air.

A few years previously we'd done a project at the Lake D'Arbonne State Park, which some local politicos had brought into being by damming the bayou. Now I crept through the quiet downtown district and found the motel that perched on the north side of the lake. I woke up the clerk, took a room, and collapsed on the bed in my clothes.

Here, in the antiseptic surroundings of the motel room,

with its institutional decor, perhaps I was safe from the ghosts.

The next morning, Saturday, I got up at nine and went to the dining room for breakfast. I ordered biscuits and asked the waitress if she'd ever heard of a minister named Thomas Wilbur.

She frowned.

"I know a Fred Wilbur. He's pastor over at Shiloh Baptist. Is that who you mean?"

"How old is he?"

"Older than me, and I'm pushing forty."

"Was his father a minister?"

She shrugged. "I dunno. I don't go to that church. They're out in the country, know what I mean."

I nodded.

It made sense. The problem was that by now the elder Wilbur might be dead. There was only one way to find out.

I paid my bill and went back to my room, where I looked up the name Wilbur in the Farmerville directory.

There was a Thomas Wilbur listed on Highway 15, north of town. I thought of calling first to announce myself and then decided I'd have better luck face to face.

The cashier told me how to get there. It was two miles past the cement plant, a frame house on the right. But I ought to call, because the old man spent most of his time fishing these days.

I found it without any trouble, a single-story structure a hundred yards back from the highway. There was a vegetable garden to one side and an ancient Galaxie in the driveway. A couple of fishing rods leaned against the wall beside the front door, along with a tackle box. I knocked on the door.

The man who answered was about seventy, with gray, crew-cut hair and a T-shirt that said *Renew*.

"Reverend Wilbur?"

He nodded.

"Yes, sir."

I told him my name. "I'm from Baton Rouge. I wonder if I could talk to you about something?"

The old man's head gave a quick nod.

"Yes, sir. You mind sitting out here on the porch? I was getting ready to untangle one of my reels."

I sat down beside him, legs dangling off the porch, while he opened his tackle box and took out a reel whose line was knotted with backlashes.

"What can I do for you?" he asked, fingers working at the tangles.

"Do you know a woman named Cynthia Jane Brown?"

I watched one tangle come loose, and he started to pick at another.

"I know her."

"She was in some trouble back in the 1970s."

"That's right." Another tangle came free.

"I wonder if you could tell me what it was about?"

The current knot was harder, and he turned the spool back a little to work at it from another position.

"Dope. Cynthia got in with some people who were selling dope."

"Was she convicted of possession or distribution?"

"I think they said possession with intent to distribute."

"Cocaine?"

"Marijuana. They didn't have so much cocaine then. There was also attempted murder, but they dropped it to assault."

"Attempted murder?"

"She stabbed one of the people she was buying it from. Turned out later he was trying to sell it to her little sister. They dropped it when she pleaded guilty."

"You seem to remember it pretty well."

The rest of the backlashes suddenly came loose, and he uttered a little sigh of satisfaction.

"Yes, sir. Always felt sorry for Cynthia Jane. Her father was a weak man. Drunkard. Cynthia fell in with a bad crowd, like a lot of 'em do. Motorcycle types. But I always thought she had something in her, something different."

"How long did she serve in prison?"

"Two years. Then she got out, and I didn't hear from her until she married that rich man, Devlin."

"You've kept up with her?"

"Not until lately."

The sickness in my belly started to creep out to the rest of my body. I wiped my face. My skin was clammy.

"Lately?"

He set the reel down and looked me in the eyes.

"She came up here a day or two ago. Looked me up. We talked a lot."

I leaned toward him, senses suddenly alert. "When exactly? Was it yesterday or the day before?"

Wilbur picked up the reel and then reached into his tackle box for a can of oil.

"Let's see, today is Saturday. She came up Thursday night, I guess, because she was here yesterday, Friday morning."

"Are you sure?"

"Sure as can be." He finished oiling the reel and spun the spool. "Is it important?"

"Very important."

Because if a man had left his house yesterday morning, he couldn't have been killed a few hours later by someone two hundred miles away.

I relaxed for the first time since I had stared into Clyde Fontenot's dead face.

"Do you know where she is now?" I asked.

He placed the reel back in his box and wiped his hands on a rag.

"I do."

I waited, ready for him to tell me it was none of my business. But he surprised me. "She's at the motel," he said. "By the lake."

"By the lake?"

"Yes, sir, that's the one."

The same motel where I was staying. I must have been so tired I'd driven right past her car in the lot.

"She's still there?"

"I think so." He got himself to his feet.

We shook hands.

"Thank you, Reverend."

He nodded. "Goodbye, Mr. Graham."

I left him on the porch with his fishing gear and drove back to town.

Marijuana in the sixties and seventies was a bigger crime than it is today. And if she'd tried to stab somebody who was corrupting her little sister, I could hardly hold that against her. But most important, she had an alibi for the murder of Clyde Fontenot, and since he had probably been killed by the same person who'd shot Douglas Devlin, she was innocent of that crime as well.

I came to the traffic signal in the middle of town and chafed as I waited for it to change. A few minutes later I turned into the driveway and wound slowly up the hill to the motel on top.

There was only a sprinkling of cars in the parking area, an Olds, a carryall of the type surveyors use, a couple of pickups.

And down near the end a Ford station wagon that I recognized. Hers.

I wheeled in beside her and jumped out before the engine had stopped turning. I hurried to the reception desk, heart pounding.

I asked for Mrs. Devlin's room, and they told me it was 250, on the other side.

So I had slept not a hundred feet from her.

I cut through the passageway and went up the steps and knocked on her door. There was no answer.

Sudden fear gripped me. What if she was inside, too depressed to come out? What if she'd taken an overdose? The minister hadn't indicated there was a problem, but people sometimes concealed things.

I banged on the door again, and a maid stuck her head out of the room next door.

"There's nobody in there. I just cleaned it."

I thanked her and went back down.

Maybe she was in the restaurant. But there were only a few tables occupied, and she wasn't at any of them. I decided to go back to my room and call Wilbur. Maybe he had some idea.

I opened my door and walked in. Something was different. I sensed it. I wasn't alone.

All at once the door closed behind me, and I wheeled around.

She was standing there in cut-off jeans, a grin on her face.

"Hi," she said.

# ▰TWENTY-ONE

"What's wrong?" she asked. "You're shaking to pieces."

"I guess it's relief," I said. "I've been scared to death."

"About what?"

I told her about Clyde Fontenot and how I figured he'd been killed for the Oswald money and watched her face pale with the shock.

"And you thought maybe I . . . ?"

"What can I say?"

She stepped back, nodding.

"I guess I can't blame you. How did you find out I was here?"

"Just a guess." I told her about how I'd found the letter from Thomas Wilbur in the trunk at the foot of her bed.

"I admit I didn't have any business snooping."

"No," she said quietly. "You didn't. But I know leaving in the middle of the night seemed pretty odd. What else did you find in the trunk?"

I explained about the photo album and then about the receipts.

"It looked to me like you were trying to figure out how your husband managed to pay off some pretty hefty debts."

"I was."

"And did you?"

"I think so."

"Was it the Oswald money, then?"

She exhaled and walked over to the bed and sat down.

"I think that's the source, yes."

"And it's still somewhere on the property."

"I think so."

"He wouldn't have taken it all and put it into his bank account?"

"Not Doug. He knew that would be a red flag to the IRS. He didn't want any records, I'm sure. No, for his purposes it would have been better to leave it right where it was and draw on it when he wanted. He would eventually have spent it all, of course. He had no sense of self-denial."

I nodded. "And the money stash is the reason you're against the dam."

"One reason." She looked up at me, her eyes beseeching. "Don't you see, Alan? I love that land. It's all I've ever had. I stayed with a bad marriage for too long. I watched my son die. I don't want it all taken away. The Oswald money would just make it possible to keep going. I don't want to be rich. But I'd like to have enough to live on. The rest, well, I'd plan to turn it over to Mr. Wilbur for children with problems."

I sat down on the bed next to her.

"Did you know Clyde Fontenot was looking for the money, too?"

"I wasn't sure. Nobody took him seriously."

"Somebody did."

She reached out for my hand, and I felt her squeezing with her own.

"My God, it almost makes you believe that . . ."

"That the kids' stories about Oswald are true. I know."

"Did I really upset you that much?" I whispered. "You had to come up here?"

"That much," she said. "The other night, when you backed off, I didn't know . . . I thought there was something I'd done. Then I told myself not to act like a slut. I had to come up here and sort things out."

"Are they sorted now?"

"For me, yes. What about you?"

"I don't know."

She took a step toward me and put her hands on my shoulders.

"Can't I help you make up your mind?"

"Probably. That's what bothers me."

"Alan, you're too good." She stepped away quickly. "She must be some woman."

"Some woman," I repeated.

I drove down to a hamburger place and got the works, double everything with a couple of orders of fries and malts and soft drinks, just in case she didn't like one or the other. When I got back, she was in a wet bathing suit, running a towel through her hair.

"They say exercise takes your mind off things," she said wryly. "Let me get dry."

She turned for the bathroom, and that was when I noticed the ugly rake-marks on her flanks.

"My God—" I started, but she wheeled to face me, so that I couldn't see. "Did Doug do that?"

She bit her lip, and for an instant she seemed like a little girl caught out.

"No," she said in a small voice. "I did."

"What?" But even as I asked, I knew she was telling the truth. "But why?"

She looked me in the eyes then, and I saw something I hadn't seen there before, something at once wild and desperate.

"Have you ever hated what you were so much you wanted to die? I guess if I'd had any guts I'd have cut my wrists. But instead I just raked my fingernails over my skin. I felt like I deserved the pain."

I thought of the long nights in the women's prison and nodded slowly. People did strange things in confinement, and who was I to judge?

"It's okay," I said and pulled her to me.

"Yes," she whispered against my shoulder. "I keep telling myself that."

It was deep into evening and we were sitting by the pool when I asked her about Timothy.

"Could he have done it, paid Oswald or been the paymaster?"

Her right hand twisted a corner of her blouse.

"Timothy was a hard man. He didn't have any use for people different from himself. I was never close to him. If he'd ever found out about my trouble with the law, he would have disinherited Doug. Timothy's people were plantation class. He was states' rights, segregationist, anti-communist, isolationist." She nodded. "Yes, if anybody could have done it, Timothy could."

"And Doug was a lot like him?"

"Douglas wanted to be, but he was the weak son. Buck was more like Timothy. Doug told me when they were growing up, Buck kept to himself and left for the Army as soon as he could. I got the impression Buck inherited Timothy's tendency toward action. Doug, the younger son, just talked about it."

"There was friction between the two brothers?"

"The normal amount. I think Doug was jealous of Buck. But Buck only came back to visit once, and that was when Timothy died, so there wasn't much to worry about. Buck wrote a couple of times a year, that's all. He didn't care about the land and he seemed to be happy with Doug managing it."

"Doug's friend was Blake Curtin," I said and waited.

"Yes. But Blake went off to the Marines. Doug," she said with barely concealed contempt, "never went anywhere."

"Has Blake ever been examined to determine the cause of his speech loss?"

"I think he went to the V.A. hospital once. They sent him back without anything definite. But let's not talk about all that. I want to forget it, at least for now."

I nodded. "Sure."

"You know, I was scared to death when I checked in here that somebody would recognize me. I thought everybody on the street would look up when I drove by and say, 'My God, it's Cynthia Jane.' But they didn't. It's so nice to know you can come home after twenty years and nobody cares." She stretched and smiled. "I guess there've been plenty of scandals since then."

"Like how you got into my room," I said.

"That was easy. Reverend Wilbur called me as soon as

you left, so I found the maid and gave her a cock-and-bull story and she let me in.''

We spent the night in our own rooms, and the next morning, Sunday, I drove back to Baton Rouge. Cyn said she wanted to stay a day or so longer, attend one of Wilbur, Jr.'s, church services, as sort of a tribute to the old man who had helped her. I had the old house to confront, because now that I had exorcised my fears about Cyn, I had only my own secret terrors to deal with. And only by dealing with them was there any hope of seeing past them to what was going on in Jackson.

It was one-thirty when I reached St. Francisville. I'd promised to be in the day before to sign a statement for Sheriff Cooney, but I figured one day didn't matter, so I stopped at the courthouse and went inside. The sheriff's office was the only office open, and when I told the woman deputy why I'd come, she gave me a funny look.

"It's Sunday," she said. "Come back tomorrow."

I left, having done my duty, and arrived home just after two. The old house still loomed menacingly on one side of the boulevard, but I was ready to confront it now.

Because now I knew: The looks on my parents' faces hadn't been because of JFK; that had been a convenient maneuver of my mind, struggling to protect me by submerging a more personal problem into something cosmic.

After all, it *had* been cosmic to me.

I remembered it all now. My parents' voices upstairs in that bedroom they'd shared for so many years. They hadn't been yelling, but they didn't have to. I'd known something was wrong as soon as he'd come in. He'd taken her by the arm, and they'd gone upstairs together that October afternoon, and I'd wondered if one of the aunts or uncles had died. I'd gone to stand outside their door and that was when I heard it.

"How could you do it?" he was asking in that same hurt tone he used when I'd trespassed in some childish way. "After all these years, with somebody I work with, a client . . .''

And she was half apologizing, half accusing, through tears. "Do you have any idea how it is every day, the boredom, never seeing you because you're always at work? I felt like I was suffocating.''

"So you picked somebody who was a client, somebody I knew? To make me look like a fool. Don't you realize by now everybody knows about the two of you?''

"I wasn't thinking. It just happened.''

And I heard the word Ernie Slagle was yelling on the playground that day as we fought.

*"Bitch."*

They had never alluded to my mother's adultery in my presence, and a month later there had been another tragedy, in the streets of Dallas, and that was what my mind had picked up and molded into my own personal grief.

My mother had died first, and he had grieved. Then, years later, I had come back to care for him in his final days, and he had never mentioned it, not even as he lay gasping, and so I never knew how it had happened, how this ideal little world I had lived in for ten years had suddenly crashed one day. I had never known who was at fault or why and how they had ultimately resolved it.

And because it had never been resolved, I left their house as it had been when they had lived there, waiting for the day when it would reappear, the crisis, and I would have to confront it and deal, at last, with the ghosts.

I went inside and looked around.

Meg had been right: It really did resemble a museum.

I went up the steps slowly, the way I had that day thirty-odd years ago, almost as if I expected to hear their voices when I got to the top, arguing behind the closed bedroom door.

I stood outside the door and then slowly opened it and looked in.

And because it was a museum and the place of every item had been stamped indelibly on my mind over the years, it took only one glance to know.

My mother's picture on the dresser had been moved slightly, and the closet door that I had left cracked open was closed. Whoever it was had been very good, but the evidence was in front of my eyes: Someone had been here while I was gone and they had searched the place.

# ≡ TWENTY-TWO

The next morning, Monday, I showed up early at Sheriff Cooney's office and got a growling lecture from him on obstruction of justice. He'd gone easy on me during that Tunica business, but, by God, there was a limit. I apologized and asked him if any progress had been made in the case. He gave me a fishy eye and shoved the statement in front of me to sign. He asked if I knew where Cyn Devlin could be found, and I suggested he try her at home.

I headed east then, passed through Jackson, and pulled in at the asylum. I asked for Dr. Childe and once more was sent down the hall.

This time he was in his office, and when I said my name, his secretary called him and told me to go right in.

When I entered, the psychiatrist was standing by the window, his lab coat open.

"Mr. Graham," he said as we shook hands. "I was hoping I'd see you again."

"Oh?"

He shrugged. "Everybody knows you found Clyde's body. I was curious about what was going on out there. I got a few details from the coroner—professional gossip, you know—but I was wondering about the rest of it. Especially since you came by the other day. You mentioned Clyde, you know." He leaned toward me like a conspirator. "Tell me, does this have anything to do with our chat?"

I shrugged. "I don't know. What does the coroner say about Fontenot's death?"

"Gunshot wound to the head. I won't bore you with the medical terms. It went all the way through and came out at the base of the neck. He'd been dead about ten hours when you found him. So somebody shot him before breakfast."

"Was anything found with him? Any kind of equipment?"

"I wouldn't know about that. What would old Clyde have had, do you think?"

"I'm not sure. Just a notion." I sat down and waited for him to do the same. Then I told him what was on my mind.

"Doctor, what's the status of hysteria these days?"

"Hysteria? You mean what they used to call conversion neurosis?"

"Whatever they call it. I seem to remember from when I took abnormal psych years ago there were cases of people who lost some physical ability—say, the ability to walk—because of a psychological trauma."

"That's true. You don't see that much of it anymore, but there are cases. Why?"

"Just a personal experience I had that got me wondering."

I was thinking of the upstairs bedroom and the anguished voices from a third of a century ago. I had shoved them into a hole called forgetfulness, but at what cost?

"I see. Well, educated people tend to be aware of such things, so they don't use that particular type of psychic defense. But any kind of trauma that makes a person have to confront some unacceptable fact—well, I'd say the potential is there."

"In other words, if a person saw something that he or she couldn't accept, this person might imagine they were blind."

"Yes, only it's more than just imagining. It's an actual inability to see. There are cases of neurotic deafness, paralysis, amnesia . . ."

Amnesia. I knew about that one.

"All to protect the person from something too terrible to face?"

"In a word, yes." He leaned back in his chair and peered

down the length of his face at me. "Are we talking about a specific case?"

"Somebody I heard about."

"You're not thinking about Oswald, are you? There wasn't anything like that about him. There are lots of labels you could give him, but it wasn't conversion neurosis."

"No."

I thanked him for his time and drove over to the Fontenot place. It wasn't something I looked forward to, but I had to find out what Clyde had wanted with me the night before he was killed.

There were cars in the drive, and I wondered if the funeral was set for today. When I came to the front door, the screen opened and a man I didn't recognize invited me in. He said he was a relative of Clyde's wife and showed me into the living room, where a few neighbors sat quietly. The only one I recognized was Dewey, from the post office.

"Aline is lying down," the relative said. "Mister . . ."

I told them my name and shook hands all around.

Dewey said, "It was Mr. Graham here found Clyde."

Six shocked faces stared at me, and I gritted my teeth.

"I'm sorry," I told them.

"Aline's taking it pretty hard," the relative said. "Pills and all."

"Sure," I said. "Well, please tell her—"

The door into the hall opened then, and a woman in a bathrobe stood wavering in the doorway. Her hair was a brown tangle, and her eyes were ringed by dark circles.

"I had to get up," she said. "There are so many things to do. Has anybody gone down to the bank? Somebody has to look in the deposit box. And there's the insurance company. They have to—"

The man who'd let me in took her arm.

"That can wait until after the funeral. You don't have to worry. Go get some rest."

She brushed his hand away and shuffled toward me.

"Are you from the insurance company?"

"No, ma'am. My name is Alan Graham. Your husband called me the night before he died. I wondered if you knew what about?"

"I'm sure it was about whatever he was doing, that craziness about the ghost. He said he was going to make us rich." She frowned. "I remember you. You were here the other day."

"Yes, ma'am."

She turned to the people on the sofa.

"Well, where is the insurance man? Did anybody call them?"

I mumbled my regrets and stepped back out onto the porch. I heard footsteps behind me and turned. It was Dewey, mopping his face with a handkerchief.

"I was looking for an excuse to leave," he said. "Poor Aline. But between you and me, she'll be better off. Clyde was crazy as a hoot owl."

"You mean the Oswald business."

"Sure. The man come here, sure. I seen him. But his ghost ain't hanging around."

"What about Timothy Devlin's?"

"Timothy's?" Dewey snorted. "I hope not. He was as mean a bastard as ever walked the earth."

"Sounds like you have some personal experience."

"He threw me off his land once. Said I hadn't no business being there. I told him I had Doug's permission, and he said wasn't Doug owned the land. Just about accused me of poaching, and me a deputy sheriff. When he died, I didn't cry."

"Why did you leave the sheriff's department?"

"Politics. It's all politics. The old sheriff retired when they indicted him, and this new one, Staples, come in. Put his own friends in the deputy jobs. Threw me out without a second thought after all those years. I was lucky the assistant postmaster job was open then. But I'm still just a glorified mailman. I deliver three days a week and stay in the office the other three. Well, at least it's got government protection." He spat. "That beats the hell out of being a sheriff's flunky."

"I hear Mrs. Devlin doesn't like Staples much, either."

"Who the hell does? He couldn't catch a cold." He squinted up at me. "I hear they want to talk to Cyn. I haven't seen her lately. When I left the mail this morning, Friday and Saturday's mail was still there.''

"Maybe she's visiting relatives," I said.

"Relatives? I always heard she was a orphan.''

I drove home, arriving at the office just before noon. I telephoned Bertha, but I was told she'd called in sick. Something about a shock. Marilyn appeared from her cubbyhole with a printout I knew was bad news and told me we only had funds for two more weeks. "After that, we won't be able to pay the mortgage on this place, much less pay people.''

I tried to soothe her. Maybe Clarence down at the bank would extend our line of credit. She gave me a disbelieving look and vanished into her cubicle. She knew as well as I did that Clarence Maloney had a heart that was all dollar signs.

My phone rang and I picked it up. Maybe it was another job.

Instead, it was a voice it took me a second to place. "Mr. Alan Graham?''

"Yes?''

"This is Gene McNair. I was calling to ask if you were free for lunch.''

McNair, the chubby little glad-hander who'd introduced me to this mess.

"Probably. What's up?''

He laughed nervously. "Well, I'd just like to sit down with you, that's all. You free?''

"I'm free," I said.

"Good. Meet me at the Nineteenth Hole at the Baton Rouge Country Club in an hour and a half?''

"I'll be there.''

He'd heard about the murder, of course, and wanted to know what was going on. Well, there was nothing to do but meet with him and tell him what I knew. What I might *suspect*, of course, was something I'd keep to myself.

I pulled into the parking area at twelve-thirty. When the country club had been built back in the fifties, it had *been* in the country, and the golf course had been surrounded by trees. Now it was an easy-off from the Interstate and there were apartments and businesses on all sides. In the eighties, another country club had been built at the very edge of the parish as part of an exclusive residential development. The old money stayed at the earlier establishment, however, and I heard even some of the founders of the later development were drifting back.

I went into the men-only dining room to the left and found McNair seated at a corner table, with the golf course visible over his shoulder through the big windows. There was another man with him who looked vaguely familiar. I walked across the room, noting a few bankers and an indecently large scattering of lawyers as I went. When I reached the table, both men were standing.

"Mr. Graham, thanks for coming." McNair shook my hand warmly and indicated the other man. "This is my brother, Senator Buell McNair."

Buell was heavier than his brother and didn't bubble quite as much, but he had the same facial features and the same receding hairline.

"Senator."

"Call me Buell, please."

We took our seats, and a waiter appeared from nowhere to take our orders. I had soup and a sandwich. The senator had iced tea and blackened fish. Gene McNair ordered a cheeseburger.

"It was a hell of a thing about Clyde Fontenot," Gene said.

"Yes," I agreed.

"I hear you found him," Buell said, his little eyes watching my face.

"That's true."

Buell took one of the small cracker packages from the basket in the middle of the table and started to unwrap it.

"Got any idea what he was doing there?"

"He told me he was looking for Lee Harvey Oswald's ghost."

Both men laughed a little too much, I thought.

"Well, I guess he found him," Gene said. "Clyde always was a strange bird."

"I hear you discovered some kind of Indian site out there," the senator said.

"That's true. Lots of flint tools, no pottery. May date to four or five thousand years ago."

"You reckon Clyde was looking for that?"

"I doubt it."

The men exchanged a glance, and Buell leaned across the table.

"Mr. Graham, I heard the Corps of Engineers has pulled the plug on your project."

"You hear right. The Corps' representative was with me when we found the body, and it scared her. She feels like it would be a big liability to the government to keep going with this unsolved."

"And if it isn't ever solved?"

"Then I guess no work gets done."

Senator Buell McNair exhaled.

"Mr. Graham, we need this project to go through. We've put a lot of money into it. And," he added as an after-thought, "it's good for the people of the area."

"Talk to the Corps," I said. "I need the job, too, but I'm just a contractor."

"I know. Your company's on pretty thin ice, from what I hear."

"Senator, any credit-reporting agency can tell you that. *I'd* have told you that."

He raised a hand. "Don't get your back up. I was just saying we've got a mutual interest."

"And?"

He chewed on the cracker, and little crumbs fell down out of his mouth.

"I may be able to get the Corps to change its mind. The governor is interested in this project. That colonel down there in New Orleans that runs the Corps district will piss in his hard hat if a congressman calls him."

"Then I wish you well."

"You're willing to go back out there?"

"With reasonable protection."

"That can be arranged."

My soup came, and the conversation changed to archaeology. Both men pretended to be interested in my field, but I could tell they'd already had the only part of the conversation they cared about.

At the end of the meal I got up, shook hands with them, and went back out into the heat. The Blazer was parked under a tree, and once I got in, I just sat quietly and ran the air-conditioning for a few seconds until the inside was cold. Then I edged out across Jefferson Highway and onto the Interstate. It was only four miles later, when I slipped off at the Dalrymple exit, that I realized I was being followed.

# ≡ TWENTY-THREE

It was a gray Plymouth, hanging a hundred yards back all the way, but weaving in and out of the traffic to keep me in sight. By the time I got to the office, it was gone. I told myself it was my imagination. Nobody had been following me. I fiddled with paperwork for an hour or so, but my mind was far away. The McNairs had invited me to lunch to find out what I knew. Buell McNair was old enough to have been a young man when Oswald had come to town. Had he known Timothy Devlin? Did he have something to hide, something that was buried on the property?

Then I remembered that Gene McNair had only bought his land a short while ago.

Suppose the entire dam project was a ploy to let them buy the land without suspicion? What if the dam deal was *meant* to fall through, to give them a chance to keep searching for the money Oswald had buried there?

But it didn't make sense. If Oswald had buried his loot, it could as easily be on the Devlin side, in which case the McNairs would have wasted their money. Besides, they stood to make far more selling the land to the state than by finding a few hundred thousand dollars in 1960-vintage bills.

But what if it wasn't money?

I sat back in my chair and tried to picture it: Oswald writing a list of the names of the conspirators and burying it somewhere on the property.

Were dead men's names worth killing for?

I gave up trying to read the report on my desk and got up. It was three o'clock, enough time for me to make it to Clinton. I probably wouldn't get anything out of the man I wanted to see, but it gave the illusion of action.

It was ten to four when I walked into the sheriff's office and asked to see Staples. He came out promptly, almost as if he'd been expecting me, looking more like a Madison Avenue account executive than a lawman.

"Mr. Graham," he said.

We shook hands, and I told him I was interested in what progress he'd made on the case. He gave me an appraising look and invited me into his inner sanctum.

The walls were plastered with framed photographs of him with different dignitaries, and I recognized a senator, a famous television anchor, and the vice-president of the United States.

"Sit down," he said.

I obliged and watched him settle into a swivel chair behind an almost obsessively neat desk.

"Hot day," he said pleasantly, like he had all the time in the world.

"Sheriff, what's the progress on the Fontenot murder case?"

"We're working on it," he said. "It's only been a couple of days."

"You told me most murders that are solved are figured out inside of forty-eight hours," I reminded him.

"That's true." He seemed undisturbed.

"And the Doug Devlin killing was never solved."

His heavy brows rose slightly. "Devlin, eh? You think there's a connection?"

"Isn't there?"

"I don't know. But I'll tell you one thing: We could make a lot better progress if we could interview everybody we had to. Like Mrs. Cynthia Devlin, for example. Know where she is?"

I realized now why she didn't like him. He was playing cat and mouse, asking questions whose answers he knew to see what response he got.

"Is there a warrant out for her?" I asked. "Is she a suspect?"

"Everybody's a suspect at this point. Haven't seen her, eh?"

"I'm told she left town—before the murder."

Staples nodded. "Beautiful woman, Mrs. Devlin. But I've always had the feeling she didn't like me."

I leaned forward in my chair.

"Sheriff Staples, have you considered that something valuable might be buried on that property? That Clyde Fontenot may have been killed because he was about to find something that was worth a lot of money?"

Staples waved the idea away. "I've heard those stories. Only thing wrong is nobody can say just what it *is* that's out there."

"How about money somebody paid an assassin a long time ago?"

"An assassin? To do what?"

"To kill the president of the United States."

I gave him credit for not blinking. Instead, he sat quietly and listened to my theory, and when I was done, he didn't laugh.

"I'll look into it," he said.

"You'll look into it?"

"What else can I say? You haven't offered me any evidence, but it's conceivable. Of course, after all this time, I'm damned if I know how I'd prove it."

I spoke quickly before I could change my mind. "Maybe I could help."

He cocked his head slightly, as if hearing something novel.

"You could help?"

"Sheriff, archaeologists help law enforcement all the time. There are lots of things archaeologists are trained to do, ways they're trained to look at things that can shed light. If I could just see your files . . ."

Staples smiled.

"Thank you, Mr. Graham, but I don't think so."

All of a sudden I felt very foolish.

I left his office with the distinct impression that I'd made a fool of myself, and maybe if I hadn't been so concerned about it, I would have noticed sooner that the gray car was back.

I saw him two miles west of town. At first he was just a dot in my mirror, and then he picked up until he was a hundred yards back. When I slowed, he slowed, too.

For a few seconds I thought of gunning my engine and trying to lose him, and then I realized it would be useless, because he could easily outrace the Blazer.

I slowed for Jackson, hoping the gray car would turn off. But instead it hung back just far enough to keep me in view. Without thinking, I floored the accelerator, hoping to surprise him, but it was useless. He caught up in a few seconds.

Ahead was the traffic light where Highway 68 entered from the south. There was nowhere to hide on 68, and I shot through the green, then slowed for town. Just ahead was the place where Highway 952 joined this road, heading north toward Mississippi. My mind raced ahead to the turnoff to our survey area. It was just three miles, and there was a curve shortly before it.

I wheeled into a hard right turn and started north along the narrow blacktop, passing the museum and the Chamber of Commerce and the ruins of Centenary College. The car behind me began to close up the distance between us.

Of course I'd played it all wrong: I should have called the State Police on the cellular. That's what I told myself now, anyway, but secretly I'd been worried they'd treat me the way Staples just had.

And whoever was in the car was just following. There was no danger in that.

I looked in my mirror and saw him now five car lengths behind.

But what if he wasn't just following me? What if he was searching for a place to force me off the road, kill me?

Then Providence asserted itself in the form of a mower crawling up the road ahead of me at the sedate speed of fifteen miles an hour. The driver, a boy of sixteen or so, did his best to keep the tractor to the right-hand side, but as he went, his towed blades scythed back and forth like a worm, periodically cutting into the oncoming lane.

I closed to a few yards behind him and then whipped around, taking the left shoulder in a cloud of dust. I heard a horn in the distance as my pursuer tried to force the machine from the road, but by now I was almost to the turnoff into the survey area. I stomped on my brakes and guided the Blazer out of the skid. Then I veered left onto the dirt track, hoping the dust would settle before the gray car got here. I bumped over the track, knowing I could make better speed over the ruts than he could, and came to the iron gate. I dismounted quickly, opened it, and drove through. Then, leaving my motor running, I jumped out again and closed it behind me. I went another mile, wondering if he'd figured out yet where I'd turned. If he had, he could only get as far as the gate, and I was hoping that when he got to that point and saw it locked, he'd figure he'd made a mistake, that I hadn't come in here at all.

Our staging area was ahead, and I stopped the vehicle and got out. I walked to the end of the road, to where the valley dipped down toward the creek. The deer stand was to my right, and I decided to go up for a better view of the trail.

The wooden rungs bent under my weight, and when I got to the square hole that was the entrance to the bottom of the compartment, I reached up to grab a handhold and felt the board give slightly.

I took a deep breath and heaved myself up into the wooden box and looked over the top of the wooden wall at the countryside.

It was a nice view, all green but for a few brown patches that were clearings, and the friendly, glistening ribbon that was the creek snaking its way through at the bottom. I shifted my weight to the other side and looked through the opening at the way I had come.

I didn't know why I was worried. There was no way to get through the gate.

I'd just wait here an hour or so and then drive out. I was already congratulating myself on having fooled my follower when there was movement through the bushes and I saw someone coming down the trail.

He wore olive camouflage, and a bush hat shaded his face. He moved lightly, like a professional stalker, and a shiver went down my spine. All my brilliance had only gotten me deeper into trouble.

The man halted twenty steps behind my vehicle, and I squinted, trying to make out his features, but he was still too far away. He seemed to be considering what course to take, and after a few seconds he made up his mind, for I saw him come around the Blazer stopping ten yards from me. I sucked myself back into the darkness of the deer stand, hoping he wouldn't think to look up here. For an eternal five seconds my heart was the loudest sound in my ears, then I heard his footsteps crunching the twigs. As I listened, the sounds grew fainter, and I chanced a look.

He was going back the way he had come, as if he'd seen whatever he needed.

I didn't like it at all.

Because in the instant before I'd jerked my body back into the shadows, I'd gotten a glimpse of his face, and it was one I knew.

It was the face of Colonel Buck Devlin.

I waited until I was sure he was gone and then decided to count to a hundred, just in case. My eyes went around the bare board walls and then across the roof, and I saw the roof was actually a flat board platform with hinges at the back. I pushed upward with my hand, and it moved. I pushed the rest of the way up, and the roof rotated upward, allowing me to stand. At the same time there was a sliding sound, followed by a clatter and crash. Something had fallen from the roof to the ground. I looked over the side and drew a deep breath.

For there below on the ground was the strange machine that Clyde Fontenot had been working on the last day I saw him alive.

# ■ TWENTY-FOUR

I clambered down the ladder to where the odd instrument lay on the ground. There was no doubt about it. It was a metal detector. Clyde figured whoever would bury paper money would protect it with a moisture-proof metal box and his machine would detect the box underground. Of course, the detector's accuracy would depend on a lot of things, such as how deeply the box was buried—the car battery suggested Fontenot expected quite a hole. And maybe the thing wouldn't work at all.

But whether it actually worked was beside the point. Its significance was that if Clyde had carried it the morning he was killed, it was probable that his murderer had killed him here, stashed the machine where he figured no one would find it, and then carried—or dragged—Clyde's body down to the creek.

I tried to think of what this added to the investigation, but nothing came through for the moment. I picked up the detector, masking my fingerprints with a handkerchief, and with the apparatus under one arm, I climbed back up the ladder and into the deer stand. Then I lowered the roof and, reaching out over the side with both hands, managed to stash the instrument back on the top.

Something was telling me to leave it where it was for now.

I looked out over the valley again and found myself wondering if the killer hadn't waited up here with a rifle until Clyde had walked by below.

Ten minutes later I was back on the blacktop and there was no sign of the gray Plymouth.

When I got back to my house, the light on my answering machine was blinking. Cyn's voice told me she hoped I'd made it home all right, and she left the number of the motel. I thought about Buck Devlin and hoped he hadn't beaten me home and checked my messages.

But I didn't think he'd had enough time. Still, there was no sense in taking anything for granted. Buck was clever and had learned things in the Army. If he'd been the one who'd broken into the office and shot Meg, it was a rare slipup because, judging from the burglary of my house, which it seemed reasonable to attribute to him, he specialized in stealth. I turned things over in my mind and then went up the steps to my parents' room. Everything was as I'd left it, the small photograph still slightly out of place, the closet door cracked open. I went to the closet then and rooted through the shoe boxes on the floor. When I found the one I wanted, I brought it out and took it over to the bed.

It was bound with string, the same string my father had tied it with when I was in high school, the same string that I had retied after I'd peeked into the box one day when he wasn't home.

I broke the rotten string and lifted off the box top. I rifled through some oily rags and lifted out the object inside.

It was an ancient Colt revolver, .32 caliber, the kind people used to keep around the house. I never knew what my father had wanted with it because there were few burglaries in those days, but I remembered him putting the shoe box in the car when we'd take long rides in the country, and once he had taken me out south of town to the levee and we'd shot at tin cans. I opened the action and spun the cylinder the same way I had that day when I was sixteen years old. The chambers were empty and the mechanism smelled of oil. I left the box on the bed and went back to the closet, standing on my tiptoes to reach far back on the shelf.

The case of cartridges was still there. There were twelve of them left, and I realized we'd fired the remainder that day long ago. The brass of the cartridges was green, and there was no way of knowing how well they'd work now. I put the box in my pocket and stuck the gun in my waistband under my shirt. I felt foolish. What was a middle-aged archaeologist going to accomplish with an ancient handgun that had never been much of a defensive weapon, anyway?

I put the gun and cartridges in the glove compartment of the Blazer and drove to a pay phone in the LSU Union building. If he had my office and home lines covered or had some way of picking up my cellular transmission, a pay phone was best. I called Cyn and she answered on the second ring.

"So what's happening down there?" she asked. "I didn't want to call your office but I've been on pins and needles."

"The answer is nothing," I said. It didn't make any sense telling her about Buck. That would come soon enough.

"I was thinking of coming home tonight."

"Better stay another couple of days. Let a few more things fall into place."

"Is something wrong?"

I told her about my lunch with the McNairs. "They're ambitious men with a lot of power. I'd hate to have them raking up your past."

I didn't say anything about the two sheriffs who wanted to talk to her. After all, if she didn't know they wanted to question her, she wasn't obstructing justice by not appearing at their offices.

"You really think I shouldn't come?" she asked, and I wondered if it was hurt I was hearing in her voice.

"That's what I think," I said. "You need to stay out of the way until this cools off."

I didn't tell her my other reason, which was that I wasn't sure I could trust myself with her a third time.

When I'd hung up, I stood there in the lobby for a long minute, with students walking back and forth past me, trying to decide what to do. If things were left in the hands of Staples and Cooney, they'd pull against each other like two kids with their fingers in a Chinese puzzle. The only way to solve this was for me to do something.

In desperation I went to the snack bar, hoping a Dr. Pepper would stimulate a few thoughts. As I went to pay, something fell out of my wallet and fluttered down to the floor. I picked it up.

*S. Norman Lawrence III, Assistant General Counsel, General Accounting Office.*

He'd offered to do anything he could.

I dialed the number on the card and waited. It was nearly four-thirty here, which meant it was five-thirty in the East. The office was probably closed.

But to my surprise the phone was answered after one ring, and I heard a woman's voice, crisp and businesslike.

"Mr. Lawrence's office."

I told her my name. "I'd like to speak to Mr. Lawrence, please."

"I'm sorry, he's in a meeting."

"Could you please leave a message? I'm a friend of his daughter's. He told me to call him at this number if I needed help. In fact, he insisted."

"Yes, sir, I'll leave a message."

"Can you tell me when he'll call back?"

"Well, I can't say, Mr. Graham. I . . ."

There was the muffled sound of voices at the other end of the line, a few clicks, and then I heard Norman Lawrence speaking.

"Dr. Graham? Is that you? I was just going by my desk and heard your name."

"Mr. Lawrence, I need your help."

"Oh?"

I told him about the murder of Clyde Fontenot.

"It was on the parish line, and two sheriffs are fighting each other over it, just like they did with Doug Devlin last year. And the State Police seem to just want to leave it alone."

"Politics and bureaucracy." He chuckled gently. "Seems like I've heard that song before. Well, it isn't a federal crime—I don't see how we could request the FBI."

I thought of Jack Kennedy's grave in Arlington, not more than a couple of miles from where Norman Lawrence was now, but I decided to keep quiet about that. I'd look like a crank if I brought it up.

"Now, if there were drugs involved, we could bring in the DEA," he suggested. "And for something being smuggled in from outside the country, there's Customs. I don't guess there's a federal fugitive so we could bring in the Marshals' Service?"

He was giving me information I already had, and I sensed he considered my phone call a waste of his time, though he was trying hard to hide it.

"There's something else you can do," I said. "If you have the contacts."

"What's that?" There was a note of caution in his voice.

"I need to get some files from the Pentagon."

"Files from who?" Now he really thought I was crazy.

I told him about Buck Devlin and how I'd been followed.

"I'd like to know where he was when his brother was killed and what kind of assignments he got in the Army."

"You suspect him?"

"He seems to be capable."

"But why would he want to kill his brother or that other man?"

"I don't know. It may have something to do with something that happened a long time ago."

"Such as?"

"A conspiracy. I don't want to say more, because I don't have any proof. In fact, it's so old there may not be anybody left to prosecute."

"Alan . . ." For the first time his voice was fatherly. "I've talked to Meg about some of this. Does this have anything to do with that Oswald story?"

I hesitated and then answered, "Yes."

I heard him blow out through his teeth.

"Jesus. And if it's Oswald, then it's Kennedy."

"Yes.

"Oh, my God." There was a long silence, and when he spoke again I could barely hear him. "You know, I met him once."

"Pardon?"

"I met Jack Kennedy. I was new in Washington, and he

made a tour of the place where I was working. I was just a law clerk. But he stopped and talked to me for a few seconds. I never forgot.''

It was a long time before he spoke again.

"There are some people I know at the Pentagon. Give me the specifics, and I'll try to get the information you want.''

"Thanks. But that's not all. Is there any way you could get me access to Sheriff Staples's files on this case?''

"My Lord, you want a lot. Well . . .'' He seemed to be thinking. "What do you know about Staples? Is he a local boy?''

"I just know he used to be with DEA.''

"DEA. Hmmmm. Well, that's a start. I'll see what I can do. Give me a day or so.''

I thanked him. "So how's Meg?''

"She wants to come back and work for you. And she may just do it.''

I told him she was welcome anytime and thanked him for the help.

The next morning I went in at nine o'clock, just in time to hear my phone ringing. It was Bombast on the other end.

"Alan, have you been complaining to people?''

"About what?''

"You know about what. I got a call from the colonel this morning, direct. He never calls anybody direct. A congressman was asking about this project.''

"What did you tell him?''

"I ask the questions.''

"What's the question?''

"Did you complain to third parties about my Stop Work order?''

"No.''

I heard her sigh, a sound like wind rushing out of an ice cave.

"Well, I guess it must be the local politicians.''

"I think that would be a good bet.''

There was a brief silence.

"So are you ready to finish the survey?'' she asked.

I started to answer, then caught myself. "Are you saying you're revoking the order?"

She cleared her throat. "I'm reevaluating the situation in light of more evidence."

"I'd have to be assured of the safety of my crew," I said.

"You mean you're refusing work?"

"No. I'm suggesting a wait of another two or three days to see if this business can't be straightened out."

"Are they about to arrest somebody?"

I thought quickly, then jumped in with both feet. "I think so."

"Well, that makes sense. I think I can sell the colonel on that." Her voice sank to a conspiratorial whisper. "Any idea who did it?"

"Not yet. But I should find out soon."

"I hope they get him," she said.

"Who says it's a him?"

"Well . . ."

*Gotcha*, I thought.

"I'll let you know what happens," I said.

"Right. Keep in touch."

We hung up, colleagues in a murder investigation.

Right.

David drifted into my office.

"Did I hear that we're on again?"

"Almost," I said.

He frowned. "What does that mean?"

"It means somebody's got to be charged with killing two people."

# ◼◼TWENTY-FIVE

It was only desperation that made me drive back to Clinton. After all, what could I expect to learn? But I was running out of ideas, and when I'd talked to Sam Pardue, he'd acted like there was something about Doug Devlin he was holding back.

Probably, I told myself, it was simply that he didn't want to speak ill of the dead. But there was always a chance it was something that would help, and I didn't have much to lose.

This time, though, I drove around in traffic for half an hour until I was sure there was nobody behind me. When I was confident I was alone, I took Plank Road north past the airport and the refinery.

Once, it had taken people a whole day to get down from Clinton and St. Francisville to Baton Rouge. Two days for twenty-five miles. They'd laid a road made of planks to help them through the mud, but many had chosen to camp north of the present city and get a head start in the morning. Now a day would take you to New York or London. Or it could take you to the cemetery, the way it had Clyde Fontenot, Doug Devlin, and Doug's son, Mark.

Mark: Something about him was clawing up at me from my subconscious.

I put the urgings aside, knowing from experience they'd emerge when ready, and concentrated on the narrow road ahead. I wanted this over with. I wanted the violence to stop and above all I wanted to lay the ghost of an assassin to rest.

Because as long as there was no answer as to why Oswald had come here, he would still live. The truth, I told myself, no matter how horrendous, had to be better than not knowing.

I reached Clinton and wondered if Sheriff Staples was in his office, plotting his next confrontation with Sheriff Cooney. Two sheriffs, as different as two men could be, and two dead men had fallen between them.

*A hell of a thing,* I told myself for the fiftieth time.

When I got to the Pardue house it was nine-thirty and already steamy hot. A station wagon and a truck were in the drive, and I wondered if the old man had finished his tree house project.

When I knocked, the door opened and the birdlike woman who'd been with him in the backyard frowned out at me.

"Is Mr. Pardue home?"

"Yes. But he's not well."

"Could I have five minutes of his time? I need to ask him something about the land he used to own."

"I don't know—"

"Angie." It was Pardue's voice, coming from deep within the house. "Is it for me?"

"You've woken him up," she accused.

"I'm sorry."

She shrugged like it was all hopeless anyway.

"Well, you might as well come in."

She showed me into the living room, and I saw him then, sitting in a stuffed chair in the dark, eyes barely open. He seemed to have lost ground since I'd seen him last, a little more life having leaked out, like air from a rubber boat.

"Who are you?" he wheezed.

"Alan Graham," I said. "We met the other day. You were fixing your tree house."

"Finished it," he said. "Finished it two days ago. It's all done. I wanted to finish it. For the grandkids, see."

"And you did," his wife assured him.

"Yeah. Now . . ."

He seemed to be dying in front of my eyes.

"Mr. Pardue, the other day we were talking about Doug Devlin and I had the feeling you were getting ready to say something. You remember what it was?"

"Doug Devlin?"

"Yes, sir."

To my surprise he nodded. "I remember."

I waited, my heart thumping.

"He bought my hunting bow," he said.

"He what?"

"My hunting bow. He bought it. A fiberglass bow, cost two-fifty new. I never used it, decided to get rid of the thing. He paid for it with two brand-new fifty-dollar bills. I wanted one-fifty and he drove me down. A man like Doug Devlin. Spent all of Timothy's money, can't even hardly pay the funeral home to bury his son, and then buys a hunting bow. What kind of a man is that?"

I told him I didn't know. He sank back into his chair, the light fading in his eyes, and I knew I'd gotten all I was going to get today and maybe forever.

I drove back toward Clinton. A hunting bow. Well, maybe it wasn't so strange. Lots of people around here were bow hunters.

The memory of Mark, Cyn's and Doug's son, kept coming into my mind, as it had on the way up. Why did I keep feeling that the dead boy figured in the case, just as his dead father and his father before him and a dead assassin were all important? What kind of sense did it make? Then I thought about the scars on Cyn's flanks and a little shiver went down my spine. I wasn't sure what sense *they* made, either.

I found Dewey in the Jackson Post Office and asked him where the Devlins buried their dead.

"Just south of town," he said and gave me directions.

I found the cemetery without any problem. It was located on a knoll, the kind Indians might have camped on. Now the place was populated by a village of gray granite stones. The postmaster had told me the Devlins were near the fence, and I walked to the far side. They weren't hard to find.

Timothy's was bigger than anything else in the cemetery, a cold, veined pillar six feet high that seemed to match the man himself. There was a cross chiseled on the left and a small American flag on the right, and below them, in letters that dared anyone to dissent:

*Timothy Bardwell Devlin*
*1900–1980*
*Patriot & Father*

My stomach turned. *Patriot.* The man who had commissioned the killing of a president? Was that the kind of man whose grave I was now facing? It said something about justice and the ability to escape it that someone like Timothy Devlin not only died of natural causes, but died honored.

I turned away to the smaller stones to one side.

*Harriet Connor Devlin*
*1903–1972*
*Beloved Wife & Mother*

Obligatory, I thought, and wondered how it must have been to have lived with someone like old Timothy.

The next stone belonged to Mark.

*Mark Connor Devlin*
*Beloved Son*
*1980–1997*

There were fresh flowers in the vase at the head of the grave, and the grass around it had been plucked short. Suddenly, with an intuition verging on certainty, I knew where Cyn had gone that night when she'd left me.

The last stone in the plot was Doug's.

*Douglas Connor Devlin*
*1948–1998*

Interesting, I thought: Son and father had the same middle name, as if Cyn had not wanted to inflict her past on her only child.

I stared down at the cold gray surface, hunting for some other inscription, but there was none. No inscription, no flowers, as if Douglas Devlin's were just another of the forgotten markers scattered throughout the place.

I drove back no wiser than I'd been when I'd come here. Cyn had loved her son, doted on him. She hadn't cared for her husband. She visited her son's grave at odd hours, because there was nothing else in the world she had to hold onto.

Then, one night, she'd come here to explain to him why she wanted to let go and to beg understanding . . .

But did any of that get me any closer to understanding who had killed Clyde Fontenot or Doug?

I went back to the office and worked until two. I looked at a couple of cost estimates, made corrections, and then read through a longish report on the project we'd done a couple of weeks back in the muddy field. The culture history section was all boilerplate, telling how the first Indian peoples had arrived in the New World and bringing them down through twelve thousand years to the present. When I got to A.D. 900, though, I stopped. That was when the bow and arrow had been introduced to this area. Before that, the chief weapon had been the spear-thrower. The bow and arrow had made hunting easier and the supply of meat more stable.

Why was the thought of Sam Pardue's hunting bow popping up to bother me?

I made a note to ask Cyn if her husband had been an avid bow hunter and thumbed through the rest of the report. We hadn't found anything, so there weren't any tables of artifact frequencies.

"I'm going home," I told Marilyn.

She said something under her breath that sounded like, "We'll all be going home soon if you don't do something," but she was that way.

When I got to the house, I started to get out of the Blazer, then halted.

There was a gray Plymouth parked across the street.

I sat with my door open for a long time, trying to decide what to do.

I was being hypersensitive. I hadn't gotten a good enough look at the car that had followed me to distinguish it from any other similarly colored car of the same make and general age. Still, it was a coincidence I shouldn't ignore.

But my experience with Staples had left me chary of calling the law. I'd feel like a fool if there was nothing to it. And besides, why would someone who was breaking the law park right across from my house? I reached into the glove compartment, took out the old revolver, and carefully loaded it with cartridges. Then I eased my door closed and walked around the side of the house to the back gate. Digger ran up to greet me and gave a little yelp of happiness. I hoped if someone was inside they hadn't heard. The dog raced to the back door, waiting for me to come. I closed the gate behind me and looked around. The old concrete birdbath still leaned a few degrees askew. A cardinal, resplendent in his red coat, fluttered up from under an azalea and cocked his head at me from the telephone line. I tiptoed up the back steps to the porch and wondered if I'd remembered to leave the screen door unlocked.

I had. I slipped in, leaving Digger outside, and made my way carefully across the boards to the back door.

Like everybody else in the neighborhood, I had an alarm system, which I'd installed after my father's death. I slipped my key into the lock, turned it slowly until I heard a click, and then pushed the door open. I reached in, punched in the alarm code, and eased the door closed behind me.

If there was someone there they were being very quiet.

I entered the hallway and stopped at the sunroom, which I used as an office. I peered in.

Computer, printer, telephone—everything seemed to be in place.

I reached the end of the hallway and looked into the

living room. Everything was in order. That only left the upstairs.

I took the revolver out of my belt, feeling foolish, and started up the stairs one step at a time, halting to listen for noises, but the old house was silent.

When I came out into the upstairs hallway, a board creaked and I froze, wondering if I'd telegraphed my presence. When there was no sound in response, I started forward again, coming at last to the door to my parents' bedroom.

Why did I always end up here? Why was it this place that drew me? I knew the secret now. Why couldn't I leave it alone? There was no one here. I was being driven by my imagination, by some stirring of the unconscious that was telling me I hadn't finished with it all just yet.

I pushed the door open and froze in shock.

Colonel Buck Devlin was sitting at my mother's dresser, arms folded, a smirk on his face.

# ■■■ TWENTY-SIX

"Better put that thing down," he drawled. "Looks to me like it's still got part of the cleaning rag in the barrel. Good way to blow up an antique."

My eyes darted down, and before I realized what had happened he was on me, twisting the pistol out of my grip. I watched him toss it onto the bed and rock back on his heels.

"I believe in the Second Amendment," he said, "but I swear there's some people shouldn't have guns."

I felt the blood flood through my face.

"What are you doing in my house? And why've you been following me?"

Devlin shook his head in wonderment.

"Damn. Here's a man who's at the complete mercy of a burglar, and instead of begging for his life, he takes the offensive. I like that."

"Answer my question. And how did you get past the alarm?"

His brows rose. He turned toward the dresser.

"You know, every time I come in this house I get a funny feeling. Sort of like the spook shows when I was little. Everything's so damned neat. It's sort of like that fellow Norman Bates in the movie. You aren't Norman Bates, are you?"

I didn't say anything.

"This mirror. There are a few smudges on it, you know that? Thumbprints. But I took your prints—they're all over

176

the downstairs—and they don't match. I'll bet these prints belong to the people that used to live here. Your parents. You haven't changed anything since they were alive.''

He gave a little shrug and then his elbow crashed into the mirror, splintering the glass so that it trickled down onto the table.

''About time a few things were changed,'' he said. ''And don't worry about getting a different alarm system. I can beat 'em all.''

''What do you want here?'' I asked, trying to keep myself from rushing him, a move I knew would be disastrous.

''It's simple.'' He came a few steps toward me and stopped. When he spoke again, his voice was a velvet whisper. ''I want *you*.''

''What?''

''You heard me. My brother and I didn't get along that good. Oh, we managed, but mainly because I was away all the time. Tell you the truth, he wasn't much of a brother. But he was all I had. Folks like us, from the backwoods, we only know one thing, and that's blood. My family's blood ran out on the ground when he was shot. I want to know who did it.''

''And you suspect me? I didn't even know your brother.''

''So it seems. But you knew Clyde Fontenot and he's dead, too. Want to try to make me believe the two aren't connected?''

I was silent.

''You seem to be into everything that's happening, so I decided to check you out. I made a little visit here the other day. And what I found made me wonder. Man your age, living in a damn crypt. I asked myself, 'Is this the kind of nut could do something and maybe not even know he did it? Or the kind who could imagine his dead mama or daddy telling him to do something?' I decided to follow you, see what you were up to. Borrowed my maid's car in case you'd noticed my Bronco. But you gave me the slip the other day. Pretty smart. And I asked myself, 'Why would an innocent man give me the slip?' By the way, where were you?''

I didn't say anything, and he took a step closer. His expression remained deadpan, but suddenly his hand shot out, connected with my midsection, and all the air rushed out of me. I crumpled onto the floor and curled into a ball.

"Not smart to piss off somebody who can make you wish you hadn't ever been born." He sat down on the bed.

The room swam, and little spots of light danced in front of my eyes. An eternity later I felt air seep into my lungs again and realized I was breathing. I dragged myself up to a sitting position.

"Now, where did you go?"

"Down the hill," I said.

"It isn't nice to lie."

His right hand clenched, and I stiffened for another blow, but it didn't come.

"Then there's my sister-in-law. Pretty nice-looking little piece. You getting some of it?"

I tried to push myself up, but his foot came out and shoved me backward.

"Steady, Bud." He got up so that he towered over me, legs apart.

"Tell me, did she ever mention anything about her little problem with the law? She's a jailbird, you know."

I said nothing.

"So she told you." He shrugged. "Oh, well. I always gave her credit for cunning. Probably figured you'd find out." He crossed his arms. "You know, I wondered if maybe she'd put you up to it—killing Doug, I mean. I wondered how far back the pair of you went. So you know what I decided to do?" He bent forward, grabbed my hair with one hand, and put his face close up against mine, so that I could smell his breath, hot and slightly sweet, like blood. "I decided to come here and see what would happen if I let you catch me inside. I decided if you were the killer, you might have the guts to do something about it. But"—he let my hair go, and my head dropped—"you haven't got the balls. You're just a grown-up Boy Scout with your shovels and machetes and arrow points."

He walked to the door.

"Maybe you and Cyn deserve each other. But watch out for her. She's a black widow."

The door closed after him, and I sat on the floor, ashamed and humiliated. I'd been terrified of the pain he'd inflicted, and that had kept me from rushing him, even as he did everything he could to force me to do it. And he had dismissed me as harmless because I *was* afraid.

I got up slowly, rubbing my solar plexus where he'd punched me, and looked at the mirror. The glass was shattered, but it could be replaced. But that wasn't the point. He had violated this house, he had violated my parents' room, and he had violated *me*. My eyes fell on the bed and the pistol, and I winced. He hadn't even considered me enough of a threat to take the gun when he'd gone.

I collapsed beside the ancient weapon and stared at the floor. I wondered what my parents would have thought if they'd witnessed this scene. But a voice in back of my head counseled me to back off. It was too easy to let myself sink into self-pity. Buck Devlin had been trained to kill and I had not. Where was the shame in that? He had come here, ostensibly, to check me out and to make me so angry that he could determine whether I was the killing kind.

But what if that was all just a lie? What if Buck had done the killings himself? What if he was using me to provide an alibi for himself? The outraged brother, pursuing his kinsman's murderer.

I had nothing to be ashamed of. That's what I told myself as I went downstairs slowly, trying to make myself stop shaking. But the rage was still in me. It had been a long time since I'd hated anyone, and that had been on the playground when I was ten and a bully had rubbed my face in the dust. But I'd managed to bloody his nose and won the fight. The vice principal had read us a lecture about fighting and had threatened to call our parents, but I had the sense that secretly he was glad the bully had gotten his comeuppance.

Now I had an urge to give Buck Devlin *his* deserts.

Except that wouldn't necessarily do anything to solve the problem at hand.

No, his best deserts would be if he had killed his brother and I could prove it.

I thought of going back to the office, but there was no

way I could face the others. David would know me well enough to realize something was wrong, and I didn't want to have to tell everyone about being disarmed and humiliated in my own home.

The only thing I could do now was go back to where it had all started, Jackson, and try to find the man who seemed to know the secrets but was unable to tell.

It was time to force Blake Curtin's hand.

I found him at Cyn's, working downstairs. He'd finished the kitchen and now he'd moved to the hallway, where he was working with spackling compound and a trowel. I could see him through the window as I stood in the backyard, up on the ladder with his back to me, smoothing, applying more of the white paste, and smoothing again. He reminded me of an automaton, tireless, working with the same movements, as if time itself were pursuing him.

I went up the steps and into the kitchen, walking quietly. His work from the last time I'd been there was already dry, and I wondered how long it would take him to fix every hole and crack in the creaky old house and decided that whenever that was, he'd probably turn to painting. He was that kind of person.

For a long time I listened to the sound of his spatula smoothing the spackling, and I tried to think of some better way to get his attention than by disturbing him. But I knew the answer before the question was fully formed, and so I walked down the hallway and into the room where he worked, knowing I was changing a life.

"Hello, Blake," I said.

He froze, and then the spatula came down slowly in his hand.

"We need to talk," I said. "It's important."

He stared at me, and for an instant I thought he was going to launch himself from the ladder.

"Listen," I said, "this thing has gone on long enough. Two people are dead. It has to stop."

His tongue flicked out to touch his lips, and he gave a little half shrug.

"I don't think you killed anybody," I said. "But I think you know what's going on."

He jerked his head violently in denial.

"It started a long time ago, didn't it? It started with Timothy Devlin. He was your friend because his son Doug was your friend. I know you didn't have anything to do with what happened back then, but thirty-six years is too long to keep it all bottled up. I know, I've been keeping something bottled up, too. And it cost me a lot of effort. Maybe we both need to let go."

His face was the color of the plaster on the wall now, and he seemed to sway. His lips opened and I saw yellow teeth.

"Two dead people are a hell of a load. You know their names, don't you?" I took a step toward him, steadying the ladder with one hand. "No, I'm not talking about Doug and Mr. Fontenot. I'm talking about the first two. You know their names . . ."

He was shaking now, and the spatula dropped out of his hand and clattered onto the floor.

"The first man was somebody we all knew. We saw him on TV with his wife. We saw him standing there without a hat when he was inaugurated. And then we saw him in that motorcade. You know his name. It was Jack Kennedy."

His mouth yawned open in pain, and he sank down onto the top of the ladder, his back falling against the surface he had just finished.

"Jack Kennedy was killed because of something that happened here, and you know it. You know the truth. You may be the only one left who *does* know the truth." I was whispering now, my face a few inches from his, and I saw his eyes were screwed shut, as if he could will it away.

"Because the other dead man was Oswald. You were here when he came. You know what happened. You've got the truth locked up inside you, and if you tell it, we can find out about the others, Fontenot and Doug Devlin."

All at once a sound rose out of him like wind on the tundra. It was a kind of howl I had never heard before, at once lonely and hopeless. He plowed past, knocking me backward, and I tripped over the ladder, grabbing it for support and feeling it fall down on top of me. It took precious seconds to disentangle myself and get back to my feet, and by that time I heard the motor of his truck starting.

I lurched after him, reaching the back door in time to see the truck disappear around the house in a cloud of dust. I ran after it, reaching the Blazer where it was parked in front of the house and then making a circle in the front yard.

Curtin had turned south, toward Highway 10, but I didn't think he had any plan—he was just running. If he continued on this road, he'd end up in St. Francisville, but even as I tried to close the gap, I saw him shoot left onto Highway 965, a narrow, tree-canopied blacktop that angled southwest. I followed for two miles and saw him swerve left again, this time onto another blacktop. This one led to Star Hill, a small community six miles to the west on Highway 61.

Maybe, I thought, he'd run himself out, like a horse that had yet to be broken. Maybe if I just kept back . . .

I tried hanging behind, but his truck only grew smaller in the distance, so I gunned to keep up. The road was narrow and shady, with curves, and I couldn't afford to take my eyes off the asphalt. There was nowhere else to go, so even if he was out of sight now, I knew he was up there.

The road bent left alongside a cemetery, and I saw the stop sign for Highway 61. Which way had he gone? Right toward St. Francisville, or left toward Baton Rouge?

If he went left, he could cross Thompson Creek and hit a road that connected with Highway 68. From there it was only ten miles to his trailer.

My best bet was that he was heading for home.

I was on a winding stretch of two-lane, curving down out of the hills and onto the floodplain. There was no place to pass and no way to see further than the next bend in the road.

I urged the Blazer a few feet from the tailgate of a station wagon and realized we were coming to the place where the road widened to four lanes at the base of the hills, swinging out over Thompson Creek in an arc. I shot past the station wagon as the road opened up and accelerated.

And then stomped on the brakes.

Because near the end of the bridge, on the West Feliciana

side, there were cars stopped and people getting out. As I slowed, I saw a black smudge of skid marks. Someone had gone across the bridge too fast, lost control, and tumbled over the side.

I pulled onto the side of the road and stopped.

I didn't have to see who it was, because I already knew, but I forced my eyes over anyway.

The pickup was upside down, the camper top crushed, and its wheels were still spinning. There was a lump of clothing on the sand at the base of the bluff. The people who had seen it were still standing beside their cars, shocked.

Finally, a couple of them started down the creek bank toward the lump of clothing that was Blake Curtin.

# ▰▰TWENTY-SEVEN

They took him to Earl K. Long, the charity hospital on Airline Highway in Baton Rouge. The emergency waiting area was crowded with the usual unfortunates and their families, and I stepped out into the parking lot with my cell phone and called for Cyn at the motel. The desk clerk said she wasn't in her room. I went back and waited until the doctor came out and told me Blake Curtin was out of danger. He wanted to know if I was family and then told me Curtin had taken a bump on the head and was resting. Aside from that and a few cracked ribs he was okay, but there wouldn't be any talking to him before tomorrow. I called Cyn again at the motel, got no answer, and drove home.

This time there was no gray car outside, and I fell onto the couch in my clothes and closed my eyes.

I'd tried to solve a couple of murders and almost ended up getting a man killed. Good work, Graham.

Maybe there were some things best left alone. I'd never believed that, of course, but now I wondered if it didn't make sense. Did innocent people have to get killed to write an end to a story that was already over? And if Fontenot had gotten in the way, well, he had known the risk when he'd trespassed. Maybe I should just go to Staples and tell him about Fontenot's metal detector and let the law handle the business, even if it meant not handling it at all. There was a gentle swish of traffic outside on the boulevard, and I remembered when I had been small, my father taking me by the hand and leading me along. The worst thing then

184

had been the possibility of stumbling over a broken piece of sidewalk, where the roots of the oaks had pushed up the concrete. Another world . . .

The ringing phone took me out of my thoughts, and I forced myself over to pick it up. Maybe, I thought, it was Cyn, telling me she was back.

"Alan Graham?" I came awake instantly. It was Norman Lawrence's voice.

"Mr. Lawrence?"

"Norman, please. Look, I've got what you wanted. It took some doing, but never underestimate the fear a voice from the General Accounting Office can instill in people." He chuckled to himself, and for once I was glad of a strong, implacable federal bureaucracy.

"You've got times and places?" I asked.

"Partly. For the rest I've got a promise of cooperation." I waited and heard paper rustling as he turned pages.

"Let's see. You wanted to know about this Buck Devlin."

"Yes." My heart started its thumping again.

"Well, a lot of it's not in the personnel records. Classified and all that. You'd need a lot more muscle than I have to get to it. But I did call a fellow at the Pentagon, and he gave me what they had. And what he said was that the records show that on the date you gave last year, Colonel Francis Devlin was out of the country."

"Out of the country?"

"In one of the Arab Emirates, to be exact. The nature of his mission isn't clear, but he was definitely there for the period you mentioned."

"If it was a spook mission, how can anybody be sure?"

"Well, because of what he got when he came home."

"What do you mean?"

"It was a medal for meritorious unspecified duties in the national interest. The medal was awarded in the White House Rose Garden by Bill Clinton."

I felt suddenly weak. Lawrence was right. The president of the United States was not going to give a man a medal for duty overseas when he hadn't really been there.

"Is that bad?" Norman Lawrence asked.

"No. Just takes out the main suspect up to now."

"Sorry. On the other, Sheriff Cooney told me to go to hell and bark at the moon—his words, but I have a promise from Sheriff Staples to help you. He said he'd open his files as a special favor."

"How did you manage that?"

"You told me he used to be with DEA, so I started with them. They let slip that he was trying to get their support as part of an application for some federal funds to fight drug problems. I told him who I was and mentioned his grant application. Fear works wonders."

"So is he going to get his grant?" I asked.

"I can't say. From what they said, the drug problem was bigger down there a few years ago, and I had the feeling they sensed he was just trying to expand his empire."

"Imagine that."

Lawrence chuckled again.

"Meg says tell you hello. It's all I can do to keep her at home. She really wants to go back."

"Tell her to come ahead," I said, wondering at the same time if there'd be any work for her or for any of us.

I thanked him and went back to sit on the couch.

Buck Devlin had seemed like a good bet. He knew how to kill without being traced, and it wouldn't be the first time one brother had killed another. I'd thought he was a good candidate from the first, and after today I wanted him more than ever.

But there didn't seem to be any way he could have done it, at least Doug's murder. That only left the others.

I got out a sheet of paper and wrote down the names.

*Sam Pardue*. True, Pardue was in poor health, but he could have killed Doug Devlin three years ago and maybe even managed to get up enough strength to kill Clyde Fontenot a few days past.

*Dr. Alvin Childe*. That didn't make any sense to me, but he was worth checking, because he belonged to the hunting club that used the Pardue land.

*Gene McNair*. He didn't strike me as the kind of man who could kill, but then how did such people look? He had a motive for keeping the project under way. But why would he have killed Doug Devlin?

*Blake Curtin.* I was on thin ice here. Curtin impressed me more as an unwilling witness than a killer. Still, he might as well be checked out.

*Adolph Dewey.* The assistant postmaster had had opportunity, but that was all that came to mind. I wrote his name, but I felt like I was reaching.

*Pat Staples.* I wrote his name and set the pencil down. Did I really suspect the sheriff of East Feliciana Parish? I wasn't sure. I only knew he'd had the means and that he was ambitious. His motive was something else.

And after I'd written all the names I could think of, I came to the one name I didn't want on the list.

*Cynthia Jane (Brown) Devlin.*

I must have drifted off to sleep soon afterward because it was dark when I woke up. The phone was ringing, and when I found it, I heard Cyn's voice.

"Where are you?" I asked.

"Farmerville," she said. "The clerk said somebody'd called a couple of times, and I figured it must be you."

"Blake's in the hospital," I said. "He had a wreck on 61."

I heard her gasp.

"Is it bad?"

"Not as bad as it should've been. He missed the bridge at Thompson Creek and ended up over the side, but the doctor says all he got was a few cracked ribs and a mild concussion."

"Thank the Lord. Where is he?"

"Earl K.," I said. "They said he can have visitors tomorrow."

"How did it happen?"

I got my courage together and told her.

"I just wanted to see where he was headed. I guess I screwed things up."

"Poor Blake," she said. "He probably didn't know where he was going. Do you really think he knows anything about Kennedy's death?"

"Yes."

"Then you have to do what's necessary to find out."

"Thanks for understanding."

"I'll leave right away," she said. "I should be home in four hours."

The next morning, Wednesday, I phoned the office to say I'd be late and got a chewing out from Marilyn for letting the business slide. I called Cyn's home, got her, and told her I'd meet her at the charity hospital on Airline in Baton Rouge. The hospital was named for a former governor who'd gone crazy while addressing the legislature, and it catered to the indigent.

Cyn met me in the parking lot, dark places under her eyes from lack of sleep, and we went inside. The nurse told us Mr. Curtin was awake but a little groggy. She said we could go in at visiting hours, so we hung around for a while until they allowed people into the ward.

He was inside a curtained cubicle, his head swathed and propped on a pillow. He was staring at the ceiling, his eyes sunk back in his skull, and for a little while I wasn't sure he was breathing. Cyn leaned over him.

"Hello, Blake," she said.

Dead eyes rolled slowly over to where she stood, and I wondered if he was going to smile, but he didn't.

"They say you got a bump on the head," she said. "But you're going to be okay. They say they're going to throw you out of here in a day or so."

His mouth opened slightly and his lips moved, but no sound came out.

"I'm sorry," I said. "I guess it was my fault. I didn't mean to spook you."

The dead eyes considered me and the mouth moved silently. Then his hands rose and he seemed to be making circling signs in the air.

"What's he saying?" I asked.

"He wants something to write with," Cyn said. I took out my notepad and handed it to him, along with a pen, and he tried to edge up in the bed to write but grimaced. I bent over and watched him trace the letters, one by one, in big, circular strokes: *O-S-W-*

My skin went cold.

*OSWALD,* he had written. *MY FRIEND.*

"Your friend?" I asked.

He began to write again, and this time I saw another name: *KENNEDY.*

"Yes? What about him?"

I watched the pen move again, afraid of what the letters would spell: *OSWALD KILLED KENNEDY.*

"Yes?"

There was no other sound in the room for us but the scratching of the pen on the paper.

He finished writing then and handed me the pad.

I made myself look down and flinched.

There was no mistaking what he had written. It was a single sentence, angling diagonally across the paper and almost spilling off the side. But the words were clear.

*JFK IT WAS MY FAULT*

# ≡ TWENTY-EIGHT

We stood in the hallway. The air was ice, and the steps of nurses moving along the corridor were hollow.

"I didn't have any idea," Cyn said, hugging her shoulders. "All these years."

"All these years," I agreed. "It's a heavy load to carry."

"Do you think he'll get his voice back now?"

"I don't know."

I was looking down at the words he had scrawled on the pad, line after line in his slanting handwriting until he had used most of the paper. I went to put the pad back into my pocket, and a piece of paper that had been caught up in its pages fluttered to the ground. Before I could see what it was, Cyn bent down and picked it up.

"What's this?" she asked.

I looked at it. It was my list of suspects.

"It's nothing," I said.

"Alan, don't say that. It's *something*. What are these names for? Is this the list of people you suspect?"

I started to answer, but didn't.

"It is, isn't it? And *my* name's on this list. Is that it? Do you really suspect me? Do you really still think I had a hand in all this?"

"No, of course not. I was just looking at logical possibilities."

"And I'm a logical possibility."

"Logically, yes."

She shut her eyes and shivered. "Oh, God."

"Cyn—"

"No. Don't say anything. I need some time to sort this out." She tried to smile, failed, and stepped back, her face frightened. "I mean, I thought I'd put all this behind me. I lived with it for years, the suspicion, feeling like half a person because of what happened a long time ago. I thought you were different, that we . . ."

"I'm sorry," I said.

"You're *sorry?*" At first I thought she was going to wade into me, but then she seemed to shrink with the hurt. "Well, so am I."

She started away from me, turning her back so I wouldn't see the tears.

"Cyn—"

"Don't say anything. I'll get a cab."

I stood there in the corridor like a poleaxed ox and watched her go.

Then I turned back toward the ward. I closed my notebook, put it in my pocket, and found my way out of the hospital.


"I figured you'd be coming," Staples said. We were sitting in his private office, and he had a quizzical look on his face. "You know, I never picked you for somebody with that kind of pull. Who the hell do you know?"

"Nobody," I said.

"Somebody from the GAO called me. Don't tell me you go higher than that." He shook his head. "Well, I've been in the game too long to argue. I may not like it, but I don't argue. Tell me something, though. Did you try the same stunt with Cooney?"

"Yes."

"Told you to take a jump, did he? Last of the old-time bosses. Runs his parish like his own little island. Doesn't want any federal aid."

"Looks like it."

"So what kind of files do you want to look at?"

"I want to see what you have on the investigation of Douglas Devlin's death. Then I'd like to see what you have so far on Clyde Fontenot. I'm especially interested in the interviews you've done with possible suspects.''

''You don't want much.''

''You asked what I wanted.''

''Yeah.'' Staples shook his head in disgust and swung his chair to the side. He punched a button on his intercom. ''Gillespie, bring in the files on the Devlin case from last year. Everything we've got.''

''Do you have a place I can read and make notes?'' I asked.

His brows arched. ''You take the cake . . .''

I didn't move, waiting.

''Okay, you can use the interview room.''

He led me out of his office and down the hall to a door. He opened it, and I saw a plain metal table and some metal folding chairs.

''This is where we beat our suspects. The deputy'll bring the files in. Don't take anything out. If you do, it won't matter *who* you know inside the Beltway.''

I started through the files at one-thirty, and it took me a couple of hours to go over what they had on the Devlin affair. I pulled out my list of suspects and made notes as I checked each person's alibi.

Buck Devlin I had already eliminated, so I put a check mark by his name.

Sam Pardue hadn't been interviewed, nor had Dr. Alvin Childe, which wasn't odd, since there'd been no reason to suspect them.

Gene McNair didn't own the property across the stream then, so nobody had come to him, either.

Adolph Dewey, the assistant postmaster, had apparently been asked about mail deliveries to the Devlin house and whether he'd seen anything unusual that day. The notation by the investigating deputy was that Dewey had been at an all-day postal seminar in Baton Rouge and had referred the investigator to one of his colleagues.

I put a check mark by Dewey's name.

Blake Curtin. He had been questioned because, as a scribbled note stated, he did a lot of work at the Devlin place. But Cyn herself had vouched for him. Which meant he could also vouch for Cyn.

And that left only one name: Pat Staples.

I closed the files and went back down the hall to the sheriff's office and told the deputy I was ready for the next load. He gave me a disdainful look and told me to go back to the interview room. Twenty minutes later, after, I figured, the deputy had drunk his cup of coffee and reread the newspaper to show me he didn't give a damn who I was or who I knew, he came in and dumped the files on the current case in front of me.

"And I'll be checking 'em all when you're done," he warned.

I read for another hour and a half, wondering what they'd deleted. There was a coroner's report, statements by myself and Bertha Bomberg, and an interview with Clyde Fontenot's wife.

The coroner's report said Fontenot had been killed by a high-velocity bullet of between .25 and .30 caliber. That left the Mannlicher-Carcano in the running, because 6.5 mm was roughly .25 caliber.

Oswald's ghost?

I skimmed through the interviews for names I recognized.

Buck Devlin was missing. Evidently, no one had thought him worth talking to. So was Dewey, the postmaster, and Sam Pardue. Gene McNair had been interviewed and claimed he was at a business lunch in New Orleans. He named his brother, a judge, and a couple of business associates. It could be checked, but I had a feeling it would hold up.

There was a note that Blake Curtin had been seen by several of his neighbors at his trailer early the morning of the murder. It would have been technically possible for him to have sneaked away, but I thought it unlikely.

There was a note that inquiries were being made as to the whereabouts of Mrs. Cynthia Jane Devlin and there was a reference to a case number. I wrote down the number and went on reading. And halted.

Dr. Alvin Childe had been seen driving slowly along Highway 952 at six-thirty on the morning of the murder. He had been spotted by a deputy on patrol, who had stopped to talk with the good doctor. Childe had confessed to being a bird-watcher, which was known to be true, and had gone on his way. The deputy had noticed a pair of binoculars on the front seat of Childe's car. Later, when questioned, Childe had stated that he had seen nothing suspicious during his drive.

I came to the name Pat Staples.

Once again, I had no way of checking his whereabouts.

I closed the interview files. There was only one folder left, and as I drew it to me across the table, I saw that it bore the case number I had copied earlier.

I opened the folder, knowing already what I would find.

It was a photocopy of an old arrest record for Cynthia Jane Brown. There was also a copy of the verdict, a pre-sentencing report from Probation and Parole, and a statement by the parole officer, stating that Miss Brown had fulfilled the conditions of her release. The final document was signed by the then governor. It was an unconditional pardon, which was standard in the case of first offenders.

I closed the file and went back to the main office.

Staples was standing just inside the counter, talking to one of his deputies.

"Well, did you solve it?" he asked.

I thought about what Blake Curtin had written and wondered how Staples would take it, but decided the time wasn't right. Maybe, I thought, it would never be right.

"No," I said. "I didn't solve it."

The sheriff tisked and shook his head. "Well, write me a letter when you do," he said.

I stopped. What was struggling to come free in my mind?

It was midafternoon and a summer storm was brewing. I drove out to the cemetery, impelled by something in my subconscious that told me it was all here and that all I needed to do was make the right connection. I walked back to the Devlin plot, but this time I went past Timothy's obelisk and contemplated the markers of his son and grandson.

Thunder rumbled over the hills, and I smelled rain. I thought about another cemetery, the one where my parents were buried. They had loved each other, I knew that now. They had lived together, fought, and hated, and for years I had thought I was the cause of their problem. It was my existence that had made my father a slave to the adding machine and my existence that had made my mother desperate not to forfeit her youth.

But in the last few days I realized I had been victim of a child's logic and that they had stayed together not because of me but out of love. Maybe it wasn't the kind of passionate love they had once had, but I remembered the tears on my father's face when my mother had been buried, and I knew now how deeply he had felt it. How deeply he *had* to have felt it.

Love.

Timothy had loved his sons, but he had loved power and wealth just as much, and because of that one son had turned out a weakling.

Douglas Devlin had loved his wife, but in a selfish way that considered only how she could enhance his manly image. They had both loved their son, who lay at my feet.

A country had loved its young president, because he allowed them to believe in something that never was—Camelot.

And it had been ended by a man who loved no one, least of all himself, and now another man was carrying self-hatred with him to his grave.

All at once, with the suddenness of a clap of thunder, it came to me how it had happened, how it *had* to have happened. I stood quietly, listening to my inner voice, recoiling at what it was telling me, and when the first raindrops came pelting down, I didn't feel them, because I was inside myself, experiencing the horror of it all. Only when lightning struck a few hundred yards away and I smelled the burning it left behind did I walk slowly back to the Blazer and take the lonely highway home.

I sat shivering in the living room, dripping water on the rug, and it didn't matter. Nothing mattered except ending it now forever.

*Write me a letter*, Sheriff Staples had said.

I went to my study, took out a piece of white paper, and stared at it. Then I rolled it into my old Smith Corona, and with the wind blowing the branches outside against the eaves of the house I wrote Sheriff Staples a letter.

# ■ TWENTY-NINE

I sat on the log in my poncho listening to the sounds of dripping around me. In the last two days there had been deluges every afternoon, and for a while I'd worried that today's storm would last into the night, ruining my plans. But the rain had quit just before six, and I had been able to negotiate the mud trail in the four-wheel drive.

Two days ago I had sent a letter to Sheriff Pat Staples.

*Dear Sheriff Staples:*

*This is far too important for a phone call, where there is always the possibility of a misunderstanding. What I have to say you have to see in black and white . . .*

When I'd finished, I'd placed the letter in a plain white envelope and typed my return address in the upper left-hand corner. Then, beside the name of the addressee, I'd written, *CONFIDENTIAL.*

I wasn't sure the letter would have the desired effect, but it seemed worth the try.

*I will be at the deer stand on the old Pardue Tract. If you will come at 8 A.M., there is something I will show you . . .*

Now all there was to do was wait, with the old .32 in my belt and a gnawing in my belly that told me I was doing

196

something foolish—that people had been killed out here twice, and that one more could easily be accommodated.

So I tried to think about other things. I thought about the rest of Blake Curtin's story, painfully scribbled out during my second visit to the hospital when I'd gone alone. It was a story about two friends who had served in the same Marine unit overseas and about how one of them had been discharged early and disappeared while the other finished out his enlistment and came home to the woods and hills of the Felicianas. It was about how one day this veteran had gone to New Orleans on a weekend and had run into his friend from the Marines standing on a corner passing out pamphlets. How they had renewed their acquaintance, and the man on the street corner had written his old friend, asking about job prospects in the tiny town of Jackson, and had been told there might be openings at the mental hospital there.

I thought about it and what had happened afterward. I remembered the face of the man in the hospital bed and I felt myself starting to tremble.

I began to breathe in and out slowly. That was all I needed now—a bad case of the shakes. My mind was wandering too much. I needed to keep my mind on the present danger. Kennedy was dead. The world had changed. It was all over, and nothing would set it right, just as nothing would ever change what had been between my parents. But Clyde Fontenot's death was an occurrence that was still happening, because the greed that had caused it was still with us and would continue to be until it was blotted away.

Something crashed in the brush downhill and I jumped. It was a branch, no doubt, weighted down with water. I wasn't afraid of the trail up from the creek, anyway; it was slick now, and nobody could scramble their way up without making noise. No. The killer I was waiting for would be coming from the east, from the direction of the blacktop. So I'd left the gate open.

I'd thought of climbing into the deer stand, where I could have a better view, but I'd realized quickly I would be a target, with no way out. Better down here, a few yards off the trail, just out of sight of the Blazer.

Another branch fell against the ground, only this time in the direction from which I'd come.

I tensed.

The only noise was the constant dripping around me, set off by the croaking of frogs down near the water.

I checked my watch. It was seven-thirty, another half-hour until the time set in the letter for the sheriff to come.

Maybe I should call, make sure. I fingered the cell phone in my pocket, then removed my hand. He'd said he'd be here. Calling wouldn't bring him any sooner.

I looked west across the valley. The red ball of the sun was balancing just over the trees. The atmosphere had cooled with the rain, but the earth was still hot and the air was full of water, so that my clothes stuck to my body.

A year ago a man had run down the hill on the far side of the valley, and when he'd reached the creek, a shot had rung out. The man had staggered halfway across the shallow stream and then fallen facedown on the other bank. A week ago another man had come down the trail on the opposite side of the valley, and when he had reached the spot where I now waited, another shot had felled him. He had been dragged to the creek and dumped in.

Two murders. But the same crime underlay them both.

I checked my watch again: seven thirty-five. I was getting antsy. If I'd read this wrong, I was going to look a terrible fool.

I shifted on my log, listening.

And a twig cracked.

I leaned forward, straining to hear.

All I heard was the dripping.

I held my breath, but when no other sound came, I started to relax.

And heard another snap.

It was closer, and this time there was no doubt, because it was followed immediately by the sound of a splash— someone stepping into a puddle. I had a sudden urge to run. This was insane. I was staking myself out here like a Judas goat. What had I been thinking to write that letter?

The footsteps were a few feet away, and then I saw his legs through the brush. They were blue.

I put my hand under my poncho and took the pistol out of my belt.

"I'm over here," I said.

The legs halted and I saw the form shift position. I stood up slowly so that my upper body was visible over the brush.

"Are you looking for me?" I asked.

He was wearing a cowboy hat pulled low over his face, and it gave such a different image that at first I thought I had the wrong man. Then he raised his head a little so I could make out his face. But my eyes were focused on the rifle in his hands.

"Is that you, Mr. Graham?" he asked.

"You know it is," I said.

His eyes squinted, like he was sniffing for a trap, but then he must have decided everything was all right because he smiled.

"I read your letter," he said and reached a hand up to tap his shirt pocket. "I got it right here."

"Theft of the mails is a serious crime, Mr. Dewey. Especially for an assistant postmaster."

Adolph Dewey shrugged. "Not as bad as murder."

"Are you going to kill me, then? Like you killed Clyde Fontenot?"

"Pretty much the same. See, Staples won't be coming out here, because he never got what you wrote. I saw it and I figured I better see what was inside." He gave a hoarse laugh. "Damn glad I did. I knew I should of taken that damned metal detector and throwed it in the river. I meant to come back for it, but I was in a hurry. I figure I wiped my fingerprints off, but you never can tell. Besides, you had it figured out, so I had to come here and take care of you. I'll take the machine when I'm done."

I shook my head. "Pretty poor pay, I'd say."

He nodded. "Ain't worth a damn. But what's a man to do? I don't know where the stuff is buried. Clyde was bragging he knew. I was following him. Figured I'd take it away when he found it. But the stupid little bastard heard me behind him, wanted to know what I was doing, threatened to say something. So I shot him. Figured if they shut down this project, maybe I'll have another chance to look."

I nodded. It was about as I'd figured.

"How much is it?" I asked.

"I'd say about a million and a half. That was what was in the letter."

"The letter from Doug Devlin to the man Staples killed when Staples was with the DEA."

"That's right. They sent notes to each other. It was supposed to be in a code, but it was so goddamn simpleminded. *My aunt sends you a million and a half kisses.* Now I ask you if that ain't the dumbest shit you ever heard of?"

"It's pretty bad," I admitted. "But how did you get onto it?"

"Rumors. I heard there was a dope ring. Some of the young people were into it, rumors, word of mouth. Then I seen Doug fixing up his place and flashing money around. Where else would he get it? So I started my own postal investigation. When all a man gets for years is envelopes with windows, you learn to pick up on the ones that don't have 'em. But how did you figure out about old Doug?"

"A bow and arrow," I said.

"What?"

"He bought one with brand-new money. I wondered where he got that kind of fresh new money, too. I'd heard there'd been a dope problem around here while Staples was with the DEA. It seemed to have stopped once he got to be sheriff. I wondered if the sheriff before Staples hadn't been looking the other way when it came to dope dealing. I remembered that the sheriff had resigned and Staples came in after a special election."

"I'll be damned." He shook his head. "But how did you figure *me*?"

"Elimination," I said. "And logic. You used to be a deputy sheriff, but you quit while the DEA dope investigation was going on. Then Staples came in and let you go. I wondered if things might not have gotten a little hot for you. Maybe you were on the take, too, and saw the writing on the wall. And the first time I met you, the others at the barbershop were joking about your steaming open letters. It seemed to me the post office was a good place to find

things out. You told me yourself the DEA had been opening mail with a warrant during the big investigation. I figured you had to know something about who was involved.''

He nodded. ''Something.''

''Then there was the mail delivery the day Clyde was
killed. Cyn wasn't home, but the mail still hadn't come late
in the day, because the box was empty and the flag was
down, unless somebody had picked it up for her. I didn't
think about it then, but later it made sense. You figured on
ambushing Clyde early in the morning, and that played hell
with your schedule. At least, that was my guess.''

''Yeah. I had to come back, clean up, take care of some
things at the office. By the time I got out her way, it was
late. But none of that's proof.''

''No,'' I agreed. ''I never had proof. Until now.''

''But that proof ain't going nowhere.''

''I wouldn't be so sure. Sheriff Staples will be here any
second.''

He frowned, the first glimmerings of doubt twisting his
features.

''What you mean? I got the letter. He never saw it.''

I struggled to keep my voice steady. *Staples should be
here by now.*

''You still don't get it, do you, Dewey? The letter was
a setup. I wanted to see if you'd take it out of the mail
when you saw who it was from. That's why I wrote about
the machine, the metal detector being here, and how I was
going to turn it over to Staples, along with the other evidence I had. It was bait, and you swallowed, hook, line,
and sinker.'' I held up my cell phone. ''I called Staples and
told him to meet me here right now.''

Dewey licked his lips and then the rifle swung up until
it was pointing at my chest.

''Get your hands where I can see 'em,'' he said. ''We're
going for a walk.''

I raised my left hand slowly, wondering if I dared bring
the pistol up quickly in my right and snap off a shot. But
he poked me with the snout of the carbine when my hands
were half raised.

''What you got under there?''

"Nothing," I lied.

"Nothing?" He reached out and flicked the poncho off my arm.

"Well, I'll be damned," he swore, reaching to take the pistol out of my hand. "You didn't expect to shoot me with that?"

I shrugged.

"You're just like all of 'em," he said. "So smart, so high-and-mighty, you think you can just walk out here and everything'll go your way. Just like Doug Devlin. He never had to work. Had everything handed to him and he still couldn't make it without selling drugs to high school kids. And Clyde. He was so smart, with all that education. Never could help but try to make you feel stupid. A college degree and he was better than anybody else around here."

"There's always an excuse for murder," I said. *Damn it, where's the sheriff? He said he'd come. Has he blown me off as some kind of crank?*

"I guess Staples fits in that category, too," I said, trying to buy time.

"Staples. You know what they call the outfit where he used to work? The Drug *Enjoyment* Agency. Bunch of phonies in suits running around playing cops and robbers. Staples doesn't know what's going on in this parish. He just sits in his office and writes reports to the feds. In the old days . . ."

"In the old days everybody had his own little sideline, right?"

Dewey bared his teeth. "Move. Unless you want to get it here."

"You mean down to the creek, so I can fall in, too, like Doug and Clyde?"

"*Move.*"

My guts went cold, and I started forward down the slippery slope.

Now I knew: Staples wasn't going to make it. It was just the two of us, Dewey and me.

I'd never been one for rough-and-tumble, but it was as clear as the stream below: Unless I did something sooner, in three minutes I would be dead.

It was halfway down that I made my play. I was on a slippery stretch, with my hand out to catch a bush, and I allowed myself to totter for an instant as I let go. Dewey came behind me, the barrel of the rifle thrusting forward as he reached for the bush I'd just released. At that second I grabbed the barrel of his carbine and pulled.

He gave a yell, and at the same instant the weapon went off, the muzzle blast deafening me. He let go, and the rifle went tumbling down the slope. I grabbed his legs, and he fell down on top of me. Locked together, we rolled down the slope toward the river bank.

I got up first and aimed my fist at his head, but he ducked and caught my hand. A foot pumped out, caught me in the chest, and sent me backward into the brush. I struggled up in time to see him yanking at the pistol in his belt. I launched myself at him, but my feet went out from under me, and all I caught was his ankles.

It was enough to send him off balance, and he went down with an oath. He came up with a rock in his hand, and it slammed the side of my head. The earth spun, and I felt myself reaching out, but there was nothing there.

Then I caught a piece of cloth and pulled.

He went over the bank with me, and we fell into a pool with a splash.

Water rushed into my mouth and I spit it out. His hand pressed down on my head, but I ducked away and grabbed him around the waist as he rose from the water. A knee came from nowhere and pain knifed through my jaw.

When I pulled myself upright from the water, he was standing over me with my father's pistol.

"End of the line," he hissed.

I looked at the water pouring from the little pistol.

"That thing hasn't been fired in thirty years," I said. He thumbed back the hammer and I closed my eyes.

Then I remembered what Buck had said:

*It's still got part of the cleaning rag in the barrel.*

He raised the pistol, squeezed the trigger, and I heard a dull pop, followed by a cry of pain. When I opened my eyes, Adolph Dewey was holding his right hand, trying to staunch a flow of blood.

"Goddamn thing," he choked. "It blew up!"

I watched him squeeze his injured hand for a few seconds and then I splashed over to the sandbar and picked up a chert cobble. I was halfway to him when I heard movement on the bank above.

"Don't think you need to do that," Staples said. "Just push him over to this side, so Cooney can't say I was out of my jurisdiction."

# ■ THIRTY

It was cool in the sheriff's office, and I was still shivering, despite the blanket they'd given me. I told myself it was from the dip in the creek, but I knew there was another reason. Staples read my statement, nodded, and asked me to sign.

"I guess that'll about do it," he said.

"Yeah."

"I'm not saying I wouldn't have cracked the case."

"Of course not."

"Cooney'll be upset. He wanted to solve it on his side of the line," Staples gloated.

"Well, Sheriff, it's all yours."

"Reckon so." He rocked back in his chair, and I thought for a second he was going to congratulate me, but he didn't.

"I guess this'll be the end of that Oswald business," he said.

"I hope so."

"From what you tell me it was all just guilt on the part of Blake Curtin."

I nodded. "He and Oswald met in the Marines. Oswald got out and went to Russia. When Curtin was discharged, he came home to Jackson. He was friends with Doug Devlin, who, as far as I can tell, avoided the draft, thanks to old Timothy."

"Timothy had pull," the sheriff allowed. "Besides, this was before Vietnam. It wasn't such a big thing."

"Then, one day a few years later, Curtin was in New

Orleans and who does he see but his old Marine buddy Oswald, standing on the corner of Canal Street, passing out pro-Cuba leaflets. He tells Oswald he's working at the mental hospital and that there're some jobs there. A few days later Lee shows up in Jackson.''

"Looking for a job," Staples said.

"Exactly. Oswald's got one child and another on the way. His marriage is at the breaking point. He can't hold down a job. To his mind maybe he just needs to get away for a little while, start over.''

"From what I read, he was always starting over.''

"Right. Curtin sends him to a few local politicians, and maybe Oswald even registers to vote. He and Curtin go to the cabin in the woods owned by Curtin's friends the Devlins. They drink some beer and relive old times. Then Oswald tells Curtin something. He admits that in April, he took a shot at General Walker in Dallas.''

I imagined the two men in the lonely camp house, Oswald bright-eyed and intense, with that quirky smile, bragging, and how Curtin must have felt hearing the words come out.

*I almost got the son-of-a-bitch. One shot. That's all it takes.*

"Curtin thinks it's just talk. He remembers how in the Marines Oswald was always bragging. The men laughed at him, called him Ozzie the Rabbit. Now he's ranting about how he can change the world.''

*You think I can't do it? Look at Lenin: One man. He changed the world. Look at Marx. Look at Jesus Christ . . .*

"And Curtin does the unforgivable: He laughs.''

*"Ozzie, you're full of shit, just like you were in the Marines.''*

"You think so?''

That glassy stare . . .

*"I know so, podnuh.''*

"You don't know a damned thing. You don't know about the time I spent in the Soviet Union. You don't know about my contacts with the KGB, with—''

*"You didn't do jack, fella. If you ever went to Russia it*

*was as a tourist. If you'd of defected to over there you'd be locked up. Besides, what do you have the Russians want?''*

*"You won't believe until you see it, will you?''*

*"See what? Look, Ozzie—''*

*"Don't call me that—''*

*"Then don't bullshit me. So you got some old piece of shit Italian rifle. You'd blow your dick off.''*

Oswald's face flushing as he rises, empty beer bottles crashing to the floor . . .

*"You won't believe till you see for yourself . . .''*

*"You got that straight. Have another beer . . .''*

"And Oswald storms out," I finished. "Curtin forgets about it until three months later when he hears about the Kennedy assassination and sees his old friend's name in the news."

Staples shook his head.

"I can see why it shook him up."

"So bad he lost his speech. I guess a psychiatrist would say it was because in his mind what he had to say was too terrible to come out."

The sheriff shrugged. "Of course, Oswald would've done what he did no matter. It wasn't Curtin's fault."

"No. And maybe he realizes that at some level. But he's like the kid who threw the rock at the street lamp just before all the lights in New York went out. It looked like cause and effect to him."

"Hell of a thing," Staples said. "But you *do* have to wonder: What if Oswald *had* stayed here, gotten a job? Maybe he wouldn't have been in Dallas that day."

"I know," I said. "It's a pretty scary thought."

"Who he might have shot instead?"

"No. I was thinking of all the other Oswalds running around out there."

It was ten-thirty when I got to Cyn's. The lights were off downstairs, but the upstairs bedroom window was lit. I rang the front doorbell and waited.

A long time later I heard movement, and then the door opened on the safety chain.

"Alan. What are you doing here?"

"Just tying up loose ends," I said. "I'm kind of cold. You got a towel?"

She hesitated, then the door closed and opened again.

"What happened to you?" she asked, eyeing my mud-spattered clothing.

"I took a dip in the creek." I told her about Adolph Dewey and how I'd trapped him and almost been killed for my cleverness.

She sighed.

"So you can throw away your list," she said, and I wondered if I heard relief in her voice.

"No, I don't need it anymore." I walked into the parlor, vaguely aware that I was tracking mud. The hallway ahead was bright and smelled of fresh paint. "Blake did a good job," I said, touching the painted surface. "Better than he had to do."

"He's a perfectionist," she said. "He's never satisfied unless he's working on something."

"Funny," I said. "Did you notice the hall really didn't need refinishing?"

"So?"

"He even put an air vent in." I pointed to the top of the wall where it joined the ceiling.

"Air vent? But—"

"I know. You have window air conditioning units and space heaters."

"Then why?"

I walked to the kitchen and pulled the footstool into the hallway. I stood on the top and grasped one of the screws to the air vent between my fingers. The screw turned. Once I'd gotten it out, I did the same with the other one. Then I lifted the aluminum vent frame out.

"What's going on?" Cyn asked. "Why are you taking it apart?"

I reached into the hole, and when I pulled it out again I had a small metal box. I placed it on the stool in front of me and opened it. It was filled with crisp fifty-dollar bills.

"Here's what's going on," I said. "I'd say there's about half a million here."

"My God. Is that Oswald's money?"

I climbed down and plucked out one of the bills for her to see.

"A 1976 bill?"

"Then what?" She seemed honestly puzzled.

"You know what it is," I said gently. "It's the money your husband stole from his partner in the drug trade. The money Doug hid in the cabin. This is what Adolph Dewey was looking for. Dewey told us all about it. Fontenot was looking for it, too. He put out the story about Oswald's treasure, but it was really *this* money he wanted. I think he figured out that Blake had it and that's why he called me."

"But Blake . . ."

"Curtin found it in the cabin. He figured out about the drug business. But he cared about you. My guess is he was saving it for you so you'd always have it. Sort of a savings account."

The color drained from her face.

"I don't want that kind of money," she declared. "Even if it costs me this place."

I shrugged. "Well, that's your business."

She frowned. "Don't you understand? It's dirty money."

"I understand," I said. "And you're probably right."

"I'm going to take it out tomorrow and burn it," she said. "I want to get rid of everything that reminds me of the past."

I nodded.

"And after that . . ." Her eyes sought mine, looking for an answer.

"After that there's still Adolph Dewey," I said.

"What about him?"

I leaned against the wall, all the fatigue of the last few hours catching up with me.

"They'll convict him of killing Clyde Fontenot," I explained patiently, as if to a child. "And of trying to kill one of my people at my office, when he thought we might have found the box. And of cutting my tires and hitting me in the head, if that matters now. But there's one thing they can't get him for."

She stared at me but said nothing.

"They can't convict him of killing Doug, because he has an alibi."

Her eyes narrowed.

"Are you sure?"

"Very."

"Then what are you saying?"

"I think you know." I shook my head, cutting her off. "And you know what? I don't really blame you. It was Mark, wasn't it? You found out he was buying some of the same stuff his father was peddling. What did you do, confront him with it?"

She shut her eyes and her fists balled. I thought of the scratch marks on her flanks, the ones she'd put there in a fit of self-loathing. I'd been wrong about her having done that years ago while in prison, of that I was sure. The marks were more recent and came from a sense of guilt over something else.

When she spoke again, her voice was so low I had to strain to hear the words.

"I found it in his room. He'd been acting funny. I used to be a part of that scene. He wasn't going to fool me. There were mood swings, sudden rages . . . Finally I nerved myself and searched his room. When I faced him, he took off in the car. That was when he had the accident. The thing of it was he'd hardly had any for weeks. If I'd just left him alone . . ."

"You couldn't tell," I said.

"I didn't say anything to Doug. He and I didn't talk all that much. Mark's dying was just about the end. But I guess it would've just sputtered on if I hadn't heard that Doug was selling the stuff."

"How did you find out?"

"Staples. He was with the DEA. He came asking questions. Said it was all routine, but I've been around cops enough to know what they're after when they come sniffing. I waited until Doug was gone and I searched his things. I didn't find anything except some new fifty-dollar bills." She pointed at the green paper on the stool. "Just like those. I knew he had to be in on it. I remembered enough from the days when I was running with the drug crowd to know fifties are the favorite denomination. And it was the only thing that made sense, the way he'd been paying off debts. I guess I'd shut my eyes up to then because I didn't want to believe it.''

I wished I didn't have to hear the rest, but there was no stopping now.

''I listened in on the phone extension one day and heard Doug talking about it to his partner, how much money they planned to make, how his partner would run some more dope up from the Caribbean and how they'd sell it here in the parish. I couldn't close my eyes anymore.'' She looked past me, and a chill ran through me. ''With those new bills turning up, I knew Doug had probably stashed the money somewhere on the grounds. The cabin seemed like a good place to look. I went there and found it.''

I exhaled. ''And that was when you decided to kill him.''

''He was an assassin, don't you see? The same as Oswald. He was killing a whole generation. He killed his own son.''

''And that's why you took his Mannlicher-Carcano.''

''He liked the Oswald story—about how Oswald had come here. He didn't remember him, probably wasn't around when Oswald came to see Blake. But he bought the rifle after the assassination as sort of a souvenir. He used to practice with it out there on the slope. Shows the kind of person he was.''

''So you decided to use the same kind of rifle another assassin had used.''

''It seemed to fit,'' she said.

I closed my eyes for a second, wishing I'd wake up. When I opened them, she was still talking.

''It took me months to get up the nerve, would you believe that? Months for it to eat me until I couldn't stand it anymore. They even busted the dope ring in the meantime, but Doug's friend never talked. He figured his part of the money would be waiting for him when he got out. Funny . . .'' She gave me an ironic little smile. ''If he'd only turned Doug in, I couldn't have done what I did and Doug would still be alive.''

''*You* could have turned Doug in,'' I said.

"He'd have been out in ten years," she said. "And my son would still be dead." She turned away from me so I couldn't see her face. "So I made up a story about a break-in at the house, so Doug would think they were after the dope. Then I stashed the rifle out at the cabin and waited for him to go check on his stash. When he came, I was there. He tried to run. And—"

"Never mind," I said. "I don't want to hear it."

"Why?" she asked, turning back to face me. "What are you going to do?"

I stared at the woman I might have loved, who had turned out to be a murderess, but whose act of murder had really been an act of justice.

"I'm going to go home and take a bath and get on with my life," I said.

"And what I just told you?"

"You didn't tell me anything." I touched her face and then let my hand drop.

"And us?"

I shook my head.

"Maybe I'd have done what you did, under the circumstances. I don't know."

"So?"

"I didn't. Let's let it go at that."

"Alan . . ."

I gave her a peck on the lips and walked out of the house.

# ▰ Epilogue

It was a Friday evening two weeks later. I'd come in from work tired, after struggling through a management summary of the work we'd just completed on the dam project. The report had been faxed to Bertha at two o'clock, but I felt sure she'd knocked off early and would whine on Monday that it hadn't reached her when it should.

I'd gotten a short letter from Pepper meanwhile, telling me they'd headed back into the rain forest to try to finish the excavation before the rains interrupted. Naturally, she'd be out of contact during that time. During the rains they'd retire to the lab in Chetumal for artifact analysis. Maybe I'd see her in August, unless I flew down sooner.

The problem was that I had a business to run and reports to write. Bertha had intimated that there were a few other delivery orders on the horizon, and if I worked at it, maybe we'd survive.

I'd settled into the living room with a pizza to watch a ball game. The Astros were beating the Braves black-and-blue, and I was starting to feel sorry for the Atlanta team, something I seldom did.

I hadn't seen or heard from Cyn since that night, and it had been a tough couple of weeks. I kept telling myself I was guilty of misprision of felony—knowing about Cyn's crime and not reporting it. But the fact of being a lawbreaker just didn't sink in. She'd fought to avenge her son, and if that meant the killing of a man like Doug Devlin, I wasn't going to be her judge.

I'd just watched the 'Stros catch Walt Weiss off first with a throw from the catcher and I was telling myself old-time baseball wasn't dead yet when I heard the door chimes.

Who now? The weekly poker game wasn't until tomorrow night, when I'd cook up a big pot of jambalaya for those who attended. Right now I wasn't expecting anyone.

Digger bounded forward and then started barking his happy bark at the door.

I pulled the door open and went weak.

"Hi," Pepper said. "You got a place I can stash my bags?"

I stepped back, speechless.

"But I thought . . ."

"Yeah, well, we finished early, and I told Eric if he wanted me back next season, he'd have to let me go right now."

She grinned and rushed into my arms, and I pulled her to me, lifting her off her feet and spinning her around.

"I don't believe it," I said.

"Why not?"

"Jesus, you look good," I said, feasting on the tanned legs, the straw-gold hair. "I missed you so much."

"Me, too."

I grabbed her hand and started for the stairway that led up to my bedroom, but she nodded at the door.

"Don't you want to close the door? And get my things in?"

"I'd rather get your things off," I said, starting to tug off her *huipil* blouse.

She kicked the door shut.

"I don't guess anybody will steal my valise."

"God," she said, after we'd kissed for an endless minute, "I missed you so much. When I thought of you sitting here, just waiting, nothing happening, while I was down there, I felt so guilty."

"And you'll pay," I said.

"Gladly," she said, dropping her blouse on the sofa. "But can't we at least put Digger out?"

I looked down at his expectant face.

"Come on, boy," I told him. "Tonight you get pizza. But I get caviar."

# ▰Author's Note

The story presented in these pages is fiction. It is based, however, on local lore. Six reputable persons in and around the town of Clinton, Louisiana, have maintained for over thirty years that Lee Harvey Oswald appeared in Clinton late in the summer of 1963, looking for work at nearby Louisiana State Hospital in Jackson. One witness swore that Oswald arrived in a car driven by a man resembling Clay Shaw, who was later tried and acquitted of complicity in the Kennedy assassination. Another testified that he saw Oswald and Shaw together with David Ferrie, another alleged conspirator. Two employees of Louisiana State Hospital testified at the Shaw trial that Oswald had filled out an application for work. The application has never been found.

In the opinion of the author, the evidence that Lee Harvey Oswald, acting alone, shot and killed President John F. Kennedy is compelling. The possible appearance of Oswald in East Feliciana Parish, Louisiana, in the summer of 1963 remains a historical enigma.

*Malcolm K. Shuman*

www.avonbooks.com/twilight

•

Visit <u>Twilight Lane</u> for all the scoop
on free drawings and premiums

•

Look up your favorite sleuth in
<u>Detective Data.</u>

•

Subscribe to our monthly
e-mail <u>newsletter</u> for all the buzz
on upcoming mysteries.

•

Browse through our list
of <u>books</u> and read chapter
excerpts and reviews.

•